# PALE HORSE OF THE APOCALYPSE

# ALSO BY MARK GREATHOUSE

**The Frontier Chronicles**

*Perilous Trails*

*Wyoming Calls*

*Longhorns North*

*Warpath*

*Hunter Vs. Hunted*

*Freedom Drovers*

*A Poison Spreads*

*Darkness Looms*

**The Tumbleweed Sagas**

*Nueces Justice*

*Nueces Reprise*

*Nueces Deceit*

*Nueces Blood*

*Nueces Grit*

*Nueces Truth*

*Nueces Legend*

**The Tumbleweed Sagas: Junior's Story**

*Lone Star Vigilante: Justice Texas Style*

*Guns on the Guadalupe: Justice on the River*

*Railroad to Perdition: Justice Rides an Iron Horse*

*The Black Gold Mob: Capping a Crime Gusher*

# PALE HORSE OF THE APOCALYPSE

JUSTICE DEFIES DEATH

THE TUMBLEWEED SAGAS
BOOK 12

MARK GREATHOUSE

**Pale Horse of the Apocalypse: Justice Defies Death**
Paperback Edition


Wolfpack Publishing
1707 E. Diana Street
Tampa, Florida 33610

www.wolfpackpublishing.com



Paperback ISBN 979-8-89567-321-8
Ebook ISBN 979-8-89567-320-1
LCCN

*Dedicated with love to my wife, Carolyn, and to our two sons, Mike and Matt.*

# THE NUECES STRIP

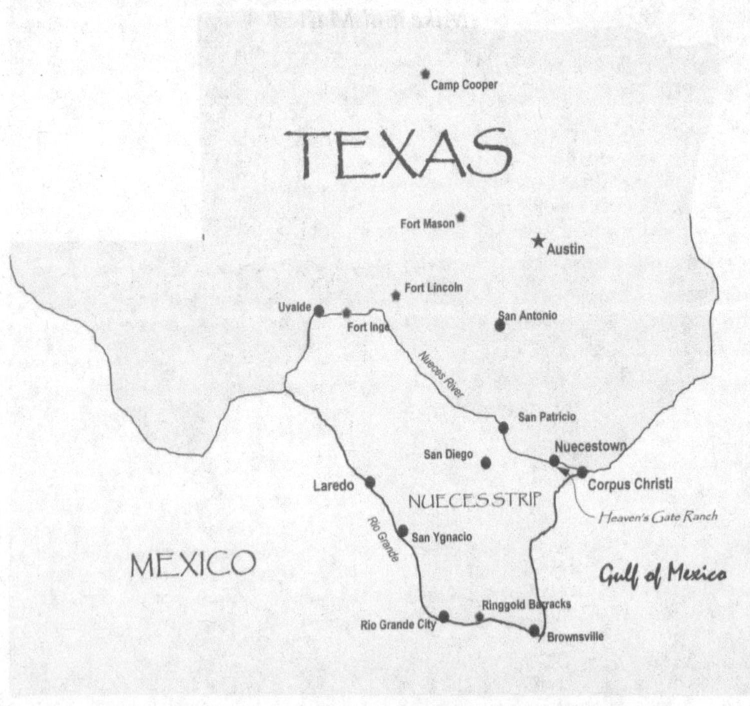


The vast Nueces Strip serves as the primary setting for the Tumbleweed Sagas. The Strip was also called Wild Horse Desert, owing to the millions of Mustangs that roamed its prairies. *(Sketch by Mark Greathouse)*

# NUECESTOWN

Nuecestown, Texas, established in 1852 by English and German settlers, was developed by Corpus Christi founder Colonel Henry Kinney along the Nueces River as a ferry crossing. Mostly thanks to the railroad passing it by, it's now a "ghost town" marked only by historical markers. All that remains is a preserved schoolhouse and the old Nuecestown Cemetery. By 1896, the town was struggling economically due to the railroads passing it by. *(Sketch by Mark Greathouse)*

# THE CAST

**Lucas Dunn Jr.**—*Goes by the nickname "Junior." The proverbial fruit doesn't grow far from the tree, as Junior follows in the lawman footsteps of his legendary Texas Ranger father.*
**Cassie McCully Dunn**—*Daughter of Grant McCully, who owns a ranch near Heaven's Gate. Cassie is married to Junior. Children are Sean, Bode, and Carolyn.*
**Elisa Corrigan Dunn**—*Widow of Luke Dunn. She'd wed Luke after losing her family to frontier rigors, including fighting off Comanche and hired killers.*
**Brody & Tess**—*Junior's blue lacy dogs.*
**Pedro Martinez**—*Ranch hand at Heaven's Gate Ranch.*
**Jimmy Donovan**—*Ranch hand at Heaven's Gate Ranch.*
**Jake Carswell**—*Former King Ranch cowboy hired as a ranch hand at Heaven's Gate Ranch.*
**Chato**—*Rogue Apache bent on avenging his oppressed people.*
**Ambrose McTavish**—*Eastern do-gooder who came west to wreak his own brand of havoc.*
**Bert Givings**—*Rancher neighbor to the Dunns.*
**Elder Barnabas**—*Leader of the Vegetarians for Life cult.*
**Max Johnson**—*Wildcatter hired as foreman for Dunn's oil venture.*
**Tochin (a.k.a. Mountain Lion)**—*Surviving and youngest son of Chato, the Apache leader.*

# HISTORICAL CHARACTERS

**Charles Culberson**—*Followed Jim Hogg and then Joseph Clay Stiles Blackburn as governor of Texas. He ran afoul of the Democratic Party over his opposition to the Ku Klux Klan.*
**John Reynolds Hughes**—*Became the longest-serving Texas Ranger captain. Hughes dealt with Comanche and Apache over his years as rancher and lawman. He was a sergeant in the Frontier Battalion down along the Texas/Mexico border until 1893, when he was promoted to captain.*
**Archer Parr**—*Known as "Archie," he established a political dynasty in what became Jim Wells County and led to decades of Democratic Party control through means fair and foul.*
**Stephen Powers**—*Political power broker exercising tight control over goings on in Corpus Christi. He has close ties with Archie Parr and Jim Wells.*

**John McTiernan**—*Sheriff of Nueces County, TX from 1896 to 1902.*
**Uriah Lott**—*Railroad entrepreneur who founded several railroads in Texas.*
**John H. Reagan**—*First chairman of the Railroad Commission of Texas.*
**Nicholas Dunn**—*Irish emigrant who came to Texas as a fifteen-year-old and settled near Corpus Christi. Legendary as a rancher, cattleman, and Indian fighter.*
**John "Red John" Dunn**—*Retired Texas Ranger who rode with Captains Wallace and McNelly.*
**Robert Kleberg**—*Married Alice Gertrudis King and became the owner of the huge King Ranch.*
**Wiley Robinson**—*Sheriff of Navarro County, Texas.*
**L.W. Cole**—*City Marshal of Corsicana, Texas.*

# THEME

## JUSTICE

*The quality of being just, impartial, or fair per the principle or ideal of just dealing or proper action in conformance to a principle or ideal as defined by the law or to truth, fact, or reason.*

# YOU'RE INVITED

Howdy,

With Tumbleweed Sagas: Junior's Story, I'm right pleased to have taken up where the story of my legendary dad left off, as he brought lawbreakers to justice as a Texas Ranger. I expect it runs strong in my ancestral blood.

*Pale Horse of the Apocalypse: Justice Defies Death* picks up my story from *The Black Gold Mob: Capping a Crime Gusher.* Like the prequels, it offers a twisted tale of intrigue in my attempt to find the psychotic member of a cult. The Nueces Strip, encompassing the southern tip of Texas, could by this time be said to be afire economically, as agriculture, railroads, communications, and black gold spawned ever greater growth. Communications? While the telegraph expanded its reach, it was the soon-to-be-ubiquitous telephone that was beginning to make its presence felt mostly in the larger Texas cities. And black gold? That's Texas crude. The "Lucas Gusher" at Spindletop Hill in 1901 near Beaumont would eventually usher in the Texas oil era. Gushers of oil would become ever more commonplace, sending geysers of money into bank accounts.

Meanwhile, forces were jockeying to take advantage of the anticipated oil boom. But, while Texas Ranger flowed in my blood, I was a rancher through and through. Cotton and oil offered opportunities, but cattle was my game.

It's 1900, and the Nueces Strip could be inhospitable six ways to Sunday. Mottes or small clusters of live oak or mesquite offered occasional shade relief on the sunbaked prairies. The often-dry creek beds and arroyos eventually filled with rainwater and emptied into Nueces Bay and... farther to the east...Corpus Christi Bay. Flash flooding was an ongoing fear. Summers? Well, they tended to be hot and humid. Weather was pretty much whatever you wanted, if you waited long enough.

The abundant animal life on the Nueces Strip featured deer, javelina, fox, coyote, lynx, black bear, and mountain lion. Armadillos and prairie dogs competed for prairie real estate. At one point, horses were more numerous on the Strip than any animal, including humans. Occasionally, spotted ocelots and even wolves could be sighted by the practiced eye. Owls, hawks, eagles, buzzards...they abounded. Come spring, wildflowers swept across much of the landscape, painted like a huge rainbow, with scarlet sage, hibiscus, daisies, poppies, lilies, and the ubiquitous bluebonnets. Groves of cypress, juniper, and palmetto could be found. Pecan trees drew their sustenance from rich soil along the Nueces River. The very name "*nueces*" was Spanish for nuts. Cactus, along with yucca and agave, abounded. The Nueces Strip surely served as God's canvas.

If you were on foot, it was advisable to keep an eye and ear peeled for rattlesnakes. They tended to blend in fairly well with their surroundings, so their rattle was often folks' first and only warning of an impending attack. The rattlesnake spawned many a "Texas-ism" like "he's so bad he has rattlesnake fangs and twice the venom" or "he's so tough, he cuddles with rattlesnakes."

The similarities between natural and human dangers were often striking. Imagine the intense yellow eyes and tense muscles of a mountain lion on the hunt. A doe looks about innocently unaware. The lion's tail twitches ever-so-slightly. Patience...of sorts. The moment of attack must be exactly right. Only that infinitesimal twitch of the tip of his tail reveals the tension as he is about to launch himself. He dares not indulge even a blink of eyes. The doe sniffs the air and dips her head to feed. The mountain lion's muscled haunches spring him forward with claws splayed. His jaws grasp the doe's neck in a death grip. In its vast silence, the Nueces Strip sucks it all in. Danger was a constant.

Application of the law could too often be horrifically fast or mind-bogglingly slow. The accused lawbreaker could as easily meet his end at an impromptu necktie party as be convicted in a court of law. Fingerprint matching and DNA databases were nonexistent. My own cousin Red John Dunn capped off a ten-year enlistment with the Texas Rangers under Captain Bland Chamberlain and later Captain Leander McNelly, with several instances of involvement with vigilante justice. Taking the law into one's own hands was expeditious but illegal and fraught with far too many instances of innocent men being on the wrong end of a rope or bullet. Dunn himself was tried twice for murder and acquitted both times.

With *Pale Horse of the Apocalypse: Justice Defies Death,* I'm right pleased to share my story of building upon my legendary father's lawman footsteps and seeking to make significant headway in bringing justice to Texas. Blood, as shed by both innocent and evil men, colors the Strip. Desperate killers, rustlers, disease, and savages are part and parcel to my life. Just about anywhere I ride, death could be reaching for my reins. While it could be said that I emulate my father in building considerable notoriety and creating enemies by virtue of my success in bringing lawbreakers to justice, I am very much my own man and have begun to establish reliable allies.

While the "Cast of Historical Characters" provides some helpful true-to-life framework to the life and times in Texas, woven into *Pale Horse of the Apocalypse: Justice Defies Death* are actual settlers as drawn from my own Irish ancestors, committed to taming the frontier. Such real-life characters, coupled with actual events, have served to reinforce the fictional setting with a strong dose of historical reality.

For anyone of a mind that the frontier had been won, they had a second think coming. The wild prairies and hills of Texas were alive and kicking, lawbreaking was very much in abundance, and what one might call the residuals of old wild west justice prevailed. It's in this setting that the need for justice remained strong for better or worse.

Kindly,
Lucas Dunn Jr.

"I looked, and there before me was a pale horse! Its rider was named Death, and Hades was following close behind him. They were given power over a fourth of the earth to kill by sword, famine, and plague, and by the wild beasts of the earth."

*REVELATION 6:8*

# PALE HORSE OF THE APOCALYPSE

# PROLOGUE

I STOOD at the top of the stairs with Smith & Wesson in hand. It had already occurred to me that Sean and Bode were in the new bedroom addition downstairs. Hopefully, they'd stay there. I prayed that the Apache didn't find them. They'd been known to be right cruel with innocent children.

More bullets flew in my direction, ricocheting wildly off the woodwork. Cassie had awakened and hurried off to settle baby Carolyn, who'd been awakened by the gunfire.

I heard screams; children's screams. My worst fears had been realized. Chato had discovered Sean and Bode.

"White man!" he hollered up the stairs in broken English, flashed an evil grin, and pointed to his prizes struggling in the sweaty grasps of two of his savages. "We kill. Make even." The Apache leader's painted face gave off the darkest possible definition of hatred, as he glared at me with eyes like a rattler's fangs oozing venom.

My sons; mere babes clutched in the hands of savages, squirmed in the glistening arms of the hostiles. They cruelly tightened their grips on my defenseless babies. I felt ever so helpless at that moment.

"Dadeeee!" screamed Sean.

An Apache's rough hand covered his innocent mouth, smothering his desperate cry.

Bode was too bewildered to be scared. At only two years old, he hadn't a full grasp of what was happening. If we all survived this, I feared he'd be scarred for life. How could I save my family? How could I rescue my sons from the clutches of these savages?

Chato glared at me with fiery contempt. A smirky sneer crawled snakelike across his mouth. It was as evil a leer as might be conjured. I saw the silvery flash of the blade he drew from the beaded sheath at his waist. He waved it in front of him as if to taunt me, tested its razor-sharp edge, then swiped it within inches of my sons' faces. "White man kill Chato son, Chato kill two sons," he threatened in his fractured English. He paused to catch my reaction, savoring the moment of his revenge.

The Apache leader stood too close to Sean and Bode to risk a shot. What was I to do?

# ONE
# SAVED!

WHEN JAKE and I had chased Chato's band off from their attempt to rustle Heaven's Gate Ranch beeves, we must have killed his son. Lord knows, there was lots of lead buzzing about like a swarm of angry bees. There was no time to aim. We simply filled the air with lead and gunsmoke to chase off the marauding Apache. Now, their retribution was at hand! Consumed by revenge, Chato's face contorted with hatred-fueled anger. Rage was manifest in violence.

Despite the blue-gray gunsmoke filling the staircase, I could make out Chato clearly enough. It felt as though I was looking at Lucifer's shadow. Desperation…mine… swept over me. He was so close, I couldn't miss. But what if I did?

An explosion! I'd heard that sound before, when hunting buffalo with my dad. A slug from a Sharps buffalo gun plowed into the side of Chato's head, blowing bone and brain across the room. His knife dropped; black eyes went empty. Chato was dead before his body thudded to the floor.

Jake Carswell had arrived from the bunkhouse armed with his prized Sharps rifle. He'd wasted no time in sizing up the situation, as he poked the barrel through a broken window, took careful aim, and squeezed the trigger before Chato could make another deadly swipe with his knife. The outcome? It had been devastating for Chato.

The Apache savages holding my struggling sons were stunned. They instantly dropped Sean and Bode. The shocked warriors, brutal in their fierceness but a moment before, were leaderless and now gripped by fear. They fell over themselves in a headlong run from the house. It roused the chickens, causing them to run around clucking their fool heads off, adding to the momentary chaos.

One badly wounded Apache lay at the base of the staircase, where I'd stepped over him to pursue the others. He arose with knife in hand and waved it toward Cassie as she descended the stairs with baby Carolyn in her grasp. The battle-crazed savage took a step toward her, then looked up with horror into the muzzle of the shotgun she drew from beneath the folds of her nightgown. Cassie calmly squeezed the trigger. She never missed a step as she followed me out the front door.

Jake sent a parting shot with the Sharps that missed, but four panicked hostiles found themselves facing Pedro and his Winchester. He'd heard the ruckus as he rode up the lane from his trip to Nuecestown. He hadn't consumed enough beer to lose his senses, and the sight before him was instantaneously sobering. His carbine belched lead at the escaping Apache, dropping two as they ran desperately for their ponies.

By this time, I'd rushed down the steps from the gallery while Cassie, with baby Carolyn in one arm and wielding the shotgun in the other, followed behind me. She looked to see that Sean and Bode were safe while I headed out in time to see two Apache manage to reach their ponies and escape. I fired a couple of shots just because I needed to.

I scanned the area for any lingering hostiles. The scene was fogged over with gunsmoke and smelled of sulfur. Silence prevailed.

*"Buenas noches, Señor* Dunn," intoned Pedro, grinning casually as he fired a couple of more rounds after the fleeing Apache.

Jake, carrying his buffalo gun, and Jimmy emerged from the side of the house from where Jake had taken the shot that had killed Chato.

I stood in the yard with legs akimbo and gun still smoking. Cassie stood behind me with our children. Sean sobbed a bit, but Bode looked stunned. "That was scary as hell," I said. "Thank God y'all were here." I turned to Jake and shook my head with relief. "Where the hell you get that cannon?"

Jake was calm as a hot hound lying in the cool shade. "Won it in a poker game a couple of weeks ago back in Corpus, Mr. Dunn."

"Well, we're sure happy you knew how to use it," I said.

Jake smiled sheepishly. "Shucks, Mr. Dunn, I never fired it before tonight."

I shook my head in mock dismay and turned to Cassie. "Sweetheart, the children can sleep with us tonight, so please take them upstairs. We'll clean up a bit around here." I gave her a hug and kissed Sean and Bode. I made sure she was inside before facing the men. "The Apache made a mess. Let's get the bodies out of sight behind the barn. The rest can be cleaned up in the morning."

The irony of the moment struck me. I'd faced all sorts of mayhem as a Texas Ranger pursuing lawbreakers, but being a peaceful, hard-working rancher hadn't immunized me from violence.

The Apache? They represented the final vestiges of the Indian wars. Their hopeless fight to preserve their old ways had long been doomed. Once-proud people had been relegated to rogue bands venting their frustrations. Treaties? Hogwash! They'd been broken again and again by both sides. Yet the waves of White settlers came, washing over them like waves lapping at sandy beaches. The likes of Chato were filled with a deadly mix of fear, hatred, and frustration, as disease racked their people, elders caved to the White man's demands, and a way of life seemed—nay, it was—doomed.

So long as there was even a hint of evil among mankind, regardless of culture or religion, there would be strife. Justice? Whose? What is justice? Who defines its bounds? When is justice just? Where is it to be found? It seems that justice can be an elusive charade. Justice won't free us from the truths of the world. And yet, in the end, it is said that truth will set you free. My dad sought to deliver justice, as have I in his footsteps. We ever strive to bring truth and justice to our world, hoping that God will heal what man rends asunder.

First thing in the morning, I helped Cassie straighten our house enough to fix breakfast. The Apache had been quite effective in wrecking anything not tied down and then some. Sweeping up broken glass was a chore, but not especially difficult. Broken tables and chairs, foodstuffs spread across the floor, and an overturned and quite busted-up cast-iron stove offered greater challenges. A chill blew through broken windows, though I'd managed to cover them with oil paper.

I poured cups of coffee for me and Cassie from the copper kettle sitting on the coals in the fireplace. With the stove wrecked, there was no brewing to be done. We enjoyed a skillet breakfast cooked in our fireplace. "Why don't you take the boys to spend a day or two with your mom or mine?" I suggested as I handed her a cup. "It's going to take a couple of days to clean this mess up," I added.

Cassie was done with shedding tears after the close call. "It might be best for the boys and Carolyn," she responded in agreement.

I sat on a makeshift bench, a board set between a couple of logs. Brody and Tess were bruised a bit but lay at my feet, absorbing the healing warmth radiating from the fireplace. "I sent Jimmy to Corpus this morning to fetch a new stove and a couple of windows. Reckon it'll take about three days and we'll have this place ready for your finishing touches." I smiled, as I knew she'd want the place organized just so.

With Cassie and the kids off to her mother's place, I could focus fully on the aftermath of the attack. I can't say that the cleanup from the attack was especially pleasant. We'd dragged the bodies of the dead Apache, including Chato, behind the barn. They were out of sight but not out of range of the aroma of violent death. As per usual, the bowels of the dead vacate. The area around the back of the barn smelled to high heaven. "Pedro, Jake, let's get to digging."

We all wore bandanas over our noses as we dug enough

graves to accommodate the five dead Apache. Despite having seen dead bodies before, I found myself horrified at the appearance of Chato with half his head gone. He no longer looked like the hate-consumed, vengeful savage that had led the attack on our home and threatened my sons.

"Won't the Apache come back for their dead?" asked Jake, recalling the Indian tradition of retrieving their dead warriors for honorable burial by the tribe.

"By the time those thieving bastards get back here, the coyotes and buzzards will have feasted. I don't think they'll be back, Jake," said Pedro.

"Pedro's right, Jake. Lord knows, we didn't need them stinking up the place." I was convinced that we'd have nothing further to worry about from the Apache. The word would get out that Heaven's Gate Ranch was too tough a target.

As we put the final shovelfuls of dirt on the graves, we heard hoofbeats and the rattle of sabers coming up the lane. A cavalry patrol trotted toward us. They were impressive in their light-brown uniforms, dark-brown knee-high boots, and campaign hats. Colt Model Single Action Army "Peacemaker" revolvers sat in their holsters, while Springfield Model 1892 rifles nestled snug in scabbards hung from their saddles. A US flag waved impressively at the head of the column. Notable, this was the 9$^{th}$ Cavalry and was comprised of what folks called "buffalo soldiers."

The unit pulled up initially before the ranch house, but upon seeing no activity, reconnoitered and found us behind the barn.

"Howdy and welcome to Heaven's Gate Ranch," I said by way of greeting.

The lead trooper looked down from his mount and made a quick scan. "Looks like y'all had some trouble," he understated. "I'm Lieutenant Smith." He placed his unit at ease and dismounted.

"I'm Luke Dunn," I said with hand extended.

We shook hands. "You that Texas Ranger guy they talk about?" he asked with a tentative smile.

"I'm afraid so," I replied. "As you can see, we've had a bit of trouble." I wanted to ask him where the hell they were when word of hostile Apache in the area had gone out.

"Chato?" he asked.

"Not anymore," I responded with a nod to the fresh graves. "Sonofabitch tried to rustle some of our beeves. We ran them off, but they came back last night and attacked me and my family. They wreaked quite a bit of damage and threatened to kill my children." I glanced at Jake and Pedro. "We ended the threat."

"How many did you bury?"

"Five," I answered.

"Sorry that we weren't here to help, Mr. Dunn," noted Smith. "Does Sheriff McTiernan know?"

"I sent one of our hands to Corpus this morning for new windows and a stove. He'll be telling the sheriff." I began to wonder where Smith was headed with his questions.

"You worked with the US Marshals office up in Dallas, didn't you?"

I gave a curious nod, obviously interested in what Smith was leading up to.

"Well, the Army has been in touch with a Texas Ranger Captain Hughes. I believe you were a Ranger under him."

"What's your point, Lieutenant?" I interjected.

"Can we step aside to talk privately, Mr. Dunn?" requested Smith.

I gave Pedro and Jake a *here it comes* look and led Smith out of earshot.

Smith's voice was a low baritone. Even as a near whisper, there was no mistaking anything he said. "What I have to say is in strictest confidence, Mr. Dunn. Is that understood?"

I nodded, dreading what was to come.

"The government deeply appreciates your fine work under cover. As you are surely aware, there is serious concern over rebellious activity by Apache and native Mexicans south of the Rio Grande. Do you catch where I'm headed?" Smith's eyes locked on mine. Perhaps, it was his dark-brown skin that made his gaze all the more penetrating.

"You're asking me whether I would go undercover for the US government," I responded.

Smith nodded.

I strove to contain the anger brewing within me. I'd expected to eventually receive some sort of request like this. It wasn't Smith's fault that he'd been ordered to deliver the request, so it wouldn't be fair to take my feelings out on him. "Lieutenant, I appreciate you fulfilling your duty by coming out here to Heaven's Gate Ranch to deliver the government's request. As I shared with Captain Hughes and promised my wife, I'm committed to ranching."

"To be clear, Mr. Dunn, you're saying that you won't take the government's offer?" asked Smith.

"I think I made myself clear," I responded.

Lieutenant Smith nodded and mounted his horse. "It was a pleasure to have made your acquaintance, Mr. Dunn." He gave a smart salute and headed his patrol up the lane from the ranch.

"What are y'all looking at?" I snapped at Pedro and Jake. "We've got work to do."

"Sorry, boss," offered Jake.

The air was a tad tense, and it was my fault. “Sorry, men. Guess that undercover request hit a nerve.”

“Let’s go get the house fixed,” said Pedro, and he headed for the ranch house.

Jake grabbed the shovels. “I’ll put these away, boss.”

All was comfortable again. I’d cooled enough that I didn’t figure to mention the government offer to Cassie.

# TWO
# APPARITION?

CASSIE and our kids moved back into the house a couple of days after the Apache attack. Jake, Pedro, Jimmy, and I had done a wonderful job cleaning and restoring general order to the house, repairing furniture, installing a new stove, and inserting new windowpanes. We even managed to clean the bloodstains from the oak plank floorboards. The place lacked only the touch that a woman's hands could deliver. I thought about prying out the lead bullets embedded in some of the woodwork, but left them in. They were evidence to share with future generations of the Dunn family.

I helped Cassie and the kids from the carriage, and Pedro led the rig off to the barn. Our dogs were their rambunctious selves, yipping and prancing at our feet. It was a sweet homecoming. I made a point of reaching the front door ahead of Cassie. I paused dramatically, then opened the door and guided her in.

Cassie's eyes swept the interior. Her jaw dropped. "It's beautiful." She beamed and hugged me tightly.

"Thanks, sweetheart," I responded. "Of course, it needs your touch. I couldn't save the drapes, and you'll have to organize the kitchen to your pleasure."

"You did a great job, Lucas," she assured me as she set Carolyn down. She told the boys to play and set about organizing her kitchen.

It was a relief to see Cassie happy. Sean and Bode seemed none the worse for their Apache experience. I expect that some loving grandmotherly attention eased any residual effect. Had they been older, they might have been scarred for life.

"Jake and I are heading to the north pasture to check fences. We shouldn't be long." Essentially, I wanted to get out of Cassie's hair so she could focus on the house. I gave her a hug and kiss and did the same for the children. I strode out with Tess and Brody nipping at my heels. They seemed fully recovered from the Apache ordeal.

When I reached the barn, Jake was waiting with horses saddled. "All back to normal, boss?" he asked.

I laughed. "Nothing's ever normal around here, Jake."

"If I may ask, did you mention the visit from the 9th Cavalry?"

"We're going to keep that our little secret," I said with a grin. "No point in raising concern unnecessarily."

"I understand. You ready to head out?" he asked.

I stroked Tornado's neck. "What say you, Tornado?" I slipped him a sugar cube, gave his nose a couple of strokes, and mounted up. "Let's see what sort of *normal* greets us up at the fence line." Riding out with Jake seemed a worthy respite from the Apache raid. There's something about the vast openness of the range that frees the soul. It seemed to me that this was true freedom.

☆☆

We rode easy-like for about two miles or so before encountering one of our perimeter fences. We'd passed a couple of dozen head of cattle grazing in the late summer sun. Nothing appeared out of the ordinary, so we turned our horses and followed the fence.

The landscape on this portion of Heaven's Gate Ranch was unremarkable. It was mostly flat, featuring grassy expanses of range dotted with occasional live oak mottes, mostly dry creek beds, a few mesquite trees, and cacti. A creek that fed the Nueces River was the only water source in the north pasture.

We plodded along. The fence was looking fine. We'd gone perhaps four miles, when I happened to glance toward a gentle rolling hill a hundred yards or so beyond the ranch property line. I pulled up. Tornado gave a snort, and his nostrils flared as though sensing danger. "Did you see that, Jake?" I said, pointing to the crest of the distant hill. Even as I said the words, whatever had caught my attention was gone.

"See what, boss?" he responded with a look at where I was indicating.

I shrugged. "Maybe I was seeing things."

"What was it?" asked Jake.

"I swear I saw a man dressed in black on a gray horse." I gazed more intently at the hill. "Maybe it was an apparition."

"A what?" Jake inquired.

"An apparition. It's like a ghost," I replied. I took another glance toward the hill. Nothing.

We rode on. The image stuck in my head, though maybe it had been an apparition. We finished inspecting the fence and turned for home. Part of me yearned to investigate that hill. In any case, it would have to be another day.

"Bugging you isn't it, boss," chimed Jake with a chuckle.

"Likely wasn't anything," I insisted half-heartedly. I said that, knowing full well that I'd head back to that hill next day. I'd seen something out there. I was sure of it.

★★

I shared my story of the sighting with Cassie, as we dressed for the day ahead.

"You saw a ghost?" teased Cassie, as she sat at the vanity, combing out her long blond hair.

I fastened my shirt, standing behind her and sharing the mirror. I laughed. "I said it was like a ghost; like an apparition. I saw it, and, next thing you know, it was gone." I buttoned the back of her dress and kissed her neck.

"So, you're going back out there to investigate?" She asked it with a tone that told me I was forever a lawman in her eyes.

I sighed. "Let's roust the boys and have breakfast." She read me well, this woman I loved.

Cassie tied back her hair, then stood. She brushed provocatively against me. "Let's eat breakfast. We'll have dessert after you return from your adventure." She winked and headed to nurse baby Carolyn. There were some duties more important than cooking breakfast for her man and young sons.

We didn't mention the ghost at breakfast. I did note that any concerns about Sean and Bode experiencing any lasting trauma from the Apache attack were dispelled, as Sean tried to get Bode to pretend that he was an attacking Indian. The war games started young with play. I hoped they'd never have to face war as adults.

After breakfast, I headed to the barn to saddle Tornado.

"Where you headed, Señor Dunn?" asked Pedro. He'd already been up and hard at work cleaning stalls.

"Heading for the north pastures. I saw something that roused my curiosity yesterday when I was riding fence with Jake. Reckon to check it out." I knew what was coming next.

"We still riding in pairs?" he reminded me. "Jake and Jimmy are checking beeves in the south pastures."

I gave him a long look. "Did Jake tell you and Jimmy what I saw?"

Pedro nodded. Of course he did. There were few, if any, secrets around here.

"Okay. Saddle up."

We were soon riding at an easy walk toward the place where I'd seen the apparition. Pedro was silent, but I could tell that he found some humor in my being caught up with a ghost.

We reached the spot after about a two-hour ride. "There's a place up yonder where we made a soft gate." I headed up the fence line. A soft gate was a place where the fence could be opened without a full gate structure to permit livestock to pass. I unhitched the wire loops, and we passed through. We were now on the adjoining Givings homestead. He was a friendly neighbor and surely wouldn't mind us entering his range.

Pedro dismounted and secured the gate. "We close, Señor Dunn?"

"Just up that hill a bit," I said with a motion toward the grassy knoll ahead. I led the way. At the crest of the hill, I looked down and smiled. There were hoofprints. My apparition had been no ghost.

Pedro saw them, too. "Is no *fantasma,* Señor Dunn.

About that time, we caught sight of buzzards flapping wings and making quite a stir near an arroyo that meandered along at the bottom of the hill.

"Wonder what has them all excited?" I mused. We knew full well that they were feasting on some dead animal. They were likely competing with some coyotes or other scavengers.

Curiosity got the best of me. "Let's see what's for lunch?" I suggested sarcastically.

Pedro smiled. He was used to my quixotic ways.

Tornado wasn't all that excited as we approached the scene. Same for Pedro's gelding. We decided to dismount and ground-hitch our horses. Horses especially tended to be put off by the odor of death. We tied bandanas over our noses.

We finally got close enough to see what the buzzards and coyotes were fighting over. It looked to be a steer. It had apparently been killed the day before. Had my ghost killed it?

I took a few steps closer to get a better look. There were more horse hoofprints in the sandy loam. A sense of violence hung around the scene. I moved closer. The buzzards were none too happy with my presence, and the coyotes snarled and yapped at me. They'd made great progress in disposing of the carcass, but I was shocked at one thing that stood out. Despite the condition of the dead steer, there was a clean cut through the bones of the chest that wasn't the result of beaks or teeth. "Pedro! Come see this!"

Pedro reluctantly moved beside me.

"Do you see that cut?" I asked, hoping he'd agree that it wasn't made by scavengers.

"What could do that?" he exclaimed.

"That took a serious cutting tool. Maybe a sword or a scythe," I postulated.

We stood there for a couple of minutes, much to the ongoing consternation of the scavengers.

I finally shrugged and led Pedro back to the horses. I took one thoughtful look back before we mounted up. That slice through the side of the steer unsettled me. Our cayuses were happy to be leaving the scene. I had to admit that there was an eerie feel about the place and could hardly blame the horses for sensing it. I began putting the pieces together. I'd seen a black-clad figure on a gray horse. Whomever it was didn't hang around to get acquainted. Today, I saw a dead steer that had been killed by a cutting tool of some sort. Were they connected? If so, why had the steer been killed? My lawman's natural curiosity was getting ever more stirred up as these questions lingered.

"Do you think the horseman killed the steer, Señor Dunn?"

"Don't know," I responded. "I wonder whether the steer was one of ours? More likely, it belonged to Givings. I couldn't make out a brand."

"It was outside our property. Maybe our neighbor's steer?" suggested Pedro rhetorically.

"I expect so. I'll have to give Bert Givings a call and let him know," I said impassively. The Givings spread adjoined the northern section of our Heaven's Gate Ranch. "Remind me later," I added, as my mind was caught up with the mysterious rider.

"Is okay to tell Jake and Jimmy?" asked Pedro.

I appreciated that he was attuned to the delicacy of my apparition turning into a real human and the possibility of the random killing of a steer. To kill cattle for no reason was akin to treason in Texas. The perpetrator was no better than any predator that killed for the sake of killing. So far as I knew, it was still a hanging offense or at least a major felony. "Go ahead, Pedro. Maybe they have some idea as to what to do next."

# THREE
# REVELATION?

PEDRO and I returned sort of quiet-like. The very idea of anyone wantonly killing livestock weighed heavily on both of us. In a way, it reminded me of the folks who killed buffalo by the thousands, taking only their hides and leaving the carcasses to rot. There were also hiders, mostly Mexicans who rustled cattle solely for their hides. Even the beaver was hunted to near extinction by trappers seeking to build their stockpiles of valuable pews.

We stabled our horses, and I headed to the house to update Cassie.

She couldn't miss my clomp of boots, as I strode into the foyer. "Did you find your ghost?" she asked with gentle sarcasm.

I shook my head and hung up my gunbelt. "Nope. However, Pedro and I found what my ghost apparently left behind."

"Well, are you keeping it a secret?" she chided.

"One of Bert Givings' beeves was killed," I replied, ignoring Cassie's teasing.

"How do you know some predator didn't kill it? There are hungry mountain lions and wolves about."

I appreciated her probing question, and it made sense. "Because the steer was killed by something sharp, like a sword or axe. It had to be something with enough heft to kill a large animal like that steer."

"You described your apparition as a black-clad figure on a gray horse," she recalled.

I nodded.

"It sounds like the Grim Reaper," she suggested.

"You don't really believe that sort of thing, do you?" I responded.

"Have you ever read the book of Revelation in the Bible?" she pressed. It was a rhetorical question. She knew that my folks drummed the Good Book into us Dunn children regularly.

"Revelation 6:8 says, 'I looked, and there before me was a pale horse! Its rider was named Death, and Hades was following close behind him. They were given power over a fourth of the earth to kill by sword, famine, and plague, and by the wild beasts of the earth.' Maybe someone thinks they're God's death horseman. Just a thought, Lucas." She locked on my eyes. She was quite serious, even deadly serious, in her theory.

I took Cassie's hand. "I appreciate what you say, but that seems far-fetched. Someone would have to be not playing with a full deck to go so far as to make themselves out to be a horseman of the apocalypse."

Cassie smiled. "Think on it, Lucas. Don't just be throwing it away."

I appreciated Cassie's viewpoint, but feared that Pedro, Jake, and Jimmy would likely laugh at the idea. "What's for dinner?" I asked by way of changing the conversation.

"Ha, Lucas Dunn. You wait and see," she gently admonished me and poured coffee into the cup I'd grabbed from the cupboard. "Dinner in about an hour. Go down to the bunkhouse and tell the boys what I suggested."

I accepted the challenge. I slugged back the hot coffee, endured the burning pain in my throat, and headed out the front door with an *I'll show you* attitude.

I strode into the bunkhouse and charged through the entry door.

The surprised men paused from their various tasks like repairing tack, braiding quirts, and sewing tears in clothes.

I laughed as I scanned the room. "I've got a serious question for y'all," I flatly stated.

"You still worrying about the ghost, boss?" joked Jake.

I shot him a killer look that wiped the smile from his face. "I'm dead serious about this. I saw what I saw, and Pedro and I saw the aftermath."

"Sorry, boss. What's your question?" asked Jake apologetically.

"Cassie thinks someone is playing as the fourth horseman of the apocalypse. What do y'all think?" I glanced from face to face. There wasn't a smirk among the men.

"It'd be plumb weird for anyone to do that, boss," offered Jimmy.

"They'd have to be *muy loco de la cabeza,* Señor Dunn," replied Pedro with a deferential shake of his head.

Jake gazed at me for a long time, as though in deep thought. "What if this ghost kills one of our beeves?" An icy chill swept through the bunkhouse.

Dang, but I hated *what-ifs*. "If that happens, everybody around these parts has a problem," I responded. "Let's keep an eye out just in case Cassie's theory is right." I hoped she was wrong; hoped that this entire business was an apparition. Perhaps I hadn't seen a rider, and the dead steer was an isolated incident. I thought back to the bands referred to as *hiders*, men who rustled and then slaughtered cattle for the hides. They'd leave the carcasses to rot. This seemed more depraved. The steer appeared to have been killed for the sake of killing. What could the purpose possibly have been?

"Lots to think on, boss," mused Jake.

"Thanks. Do let me know if y'all see anything suspicious." With that, I headed back to the house.

"What did they say?" Cassie asked immediately upon my entering the house.

I sighed. "They didn't disagree with you."

"And?" she pressed.

"We're going to be on the lookout in case one of our own beeves turns up killed."

Cassie simply nodded. She wouldn't rub it in that her Revelation theory had merit.

# FOUR
# DEAD STEER

"YOU BE NEW IN TOWN," observed the barkeeper at Schilo's Saloon in Beeville. He had already seen the man's horse. It stood out by virtue of its pale gray color; uncommon in these parts.

The black-clad figure returned an icy stare.

"Friendly sort," murmured the barkeep under his breath.

The man took a deck of cards from his pocket and began to play Solitaire as he sipped a whiskey. He snapped each card loudly against the table. He finally looked up and raised his empty glass. "I'll take another, lad," he groused at the barkeep.

The barkeep brought a bottle over and refilled the man's glass. "You from back east?" he inquired, friendly-like, trying to place the patron's accent. He took a long gander at the man's cards. The decorative backs of the cards were of a custom design.

The man delivered a jaundiced sneer in response. "None of your damned business," snarled the gloomily disposed patron. He snapped another card and stared at it. "Damn!" He swiftly gathered the cards and shuffled the deck.

The barkeep shrugged. The man's voice held an accent that was strange to him. He'd spoken with plenty of folks, but couldn't place the voice. He turned to head back to cleaning glasses behind the bar, then paused. "You hungry? We got some fine steak."

The man snapped down another card. "Damn your bloodlust. What else you got?" he growled.

"Er…taters…collards…corn," suggested the barkeep timidly.

"Taters?" asked the man.

"Potatoes," the barkeep responded, curious that this man didn't know what a *tater* was.

"How quaint." The black-clad man paused. "That'll do."

"You don't like beef?" ventured the barkeep.

He received a cold sneer in reply. The man played another card.

"I'll fetch them right away," the barkeep replied with relief and scurried off to the kitchen. He glanced over his shoulder as the man revealed a strange, tight-lipped grin and snapped down another card. The man's very presence burned its way into the barkeep's conscious. Something didn't seem right with this character from back east.

★★

"We'll be rounding up a few dozen yearlings tomorrow for tagging," I said to Cassie. We'd begun placing tags on the ears of our beeves instead of branding. We'd also be castrating a few bulls, but I chose not to mention that at dinner. They'd put on more weight as steers.

"Sounds as though you'll have a busy couple of days,

Lucas. How about if I put together a feast or two worthy of hard-working cowboys?"

"You'll make our days, sweetheart," I replied with a hungry swipe of my tongue across my lips. I could tell from her smile that she had some special treat in mind.

This sure was a far cry from chasing down lawbreakers for the Texas Rangers. Tagging and castrating these days was a lot easier than when my dad had to wrestle the cattle to get them branded and turned into steers. Still, there were likely folks who thought the whole process was barbaric. I suspected that it didn't stop them from enjoying a thick, juicy steak loaded with all the fixings. "I'm going to get the men together and go over tomorrow's plan," I added. With that, I finished my coffee, kissed Cassie, and headed out.

Jake was waiting for me with a concerned expression writ large on his face.

"What's up, Jake? You look like you lost your best hoss," I chided.

"We lost a steer, boss."

"Lost?" I asked, knowing full well what he meant.

"Jimmy and I found it. Same as the cow on the Givings spread," he ruefully noted.

"Where?" I queried.

"Not far from the other one. Only this kill was fresher. We got ahead of the coyotes, boss. Jimmy and I hooked up the wagon and hauled it back here to butcher. Reckoned you'd want to see it," he concluded.

I followed Jake, Jimmy, and Pedro to the rear of the barn. I peered into the wagon. There was no doubt that the steer had been killed, as there was a deep gash through its side. Nothing natural could have made such a cut. My lawman brain kicked in. "Somebody is sending a message, men."

"Let's find the sonofabitch and hang him, boss," urged Jimmy.

I sighed. "We're not vigilantes, Jimmy. We've got to follow the law." I said the words as part of me wanted to dust off my Texas Ranger badge and go hunt the perpetrator down. I took a long look at the steer. What depraved sort would do such a thing?

"What sort of *criatura malvada* does such a thing, Señor Dunn?" lamented Pedro, echoing my very thoughts. "He be *muy loco*."

It took all I had to control my anger born of frustration. I took a deep breath. "Y'all butcher this steer while I go and call Sheriff McTiernan," I said. "We still have work to do tomorrow." I had to be a voice of calm and reason in this sudden storm. I strode purposefully back to the house.

I swung open the front door, stepped through, and slammed it shut.

The boys looked up with stunned expressions.

"What's wrong?" asked Cassie.

"The damned sonof…" I paused. The boys wouldn't understand cussing at their age, but I respected Cassie far too much. "Somebody killed one of our steers," I blurted, sending a fist crashing down on the kitchen table. I sat and breathed heavily. "The boys got it soon enough to save the meat."

"What are we going to do?" Cassie said urgently.

"I'm going to call McTiernan, then head out with Jake to see whether we can find any clues." The lawman in me had begun to kick in. I'd handle this like an investigation. I headed for the telephone.

I picked up the receiver. "Millie, put me in touch with Sheriff McTiernan." I listened to some clicks and the buzz of a phone ringing. It sounded far away. I wondered whether this technology would ever catch on.

"Hello?" It was McTiernan's voice.

I'd been lucky to catch him in. "Sheriff, this is Luke Dunn," I said by way of greeting. It was strange to be talking to someone and not seeing their face. Of course, he'd already been told who was calling.

"Junior! Good to hear from you." He knew full well that I wouldn't use this telephone contraption unless there was a serious problem.

"Somebody around here is killing our beeves." I let that hang a minute. "The Givings spread and mine have been hit. Don't know about any others."

"Killing cattle?" questioned McTiernan.

"You heard right. They're using a sword or something. Beeves had deep cuts in them."

There was a pause. "All right if I ride out there in the morning, Junior?"

"There's not much to see, Sheriff. I'm heading out to where one of my hands found the carcass of one of ours."

"Tell you what. I'll leave now. I need to visit Nuecestown anyway." He was saying that he wanted to visit the scene of the killing before the evidence was messed up. Had he forgotten that I'd been a Texas Ranger until recently? I supposed it was his way of relating to our plight. "See you in a couple of hours," he said and hung up.

"What did he say?" asked Cassie.

"He's heading out here. We'll wait for him. Hopefully, we can search the scene before dark."

Cassie set a steaming cup of coffee in front of me. She gave me *that* look. "You're heading out there now, aren't you?"

I nodded sheepishly. There was no way that I was going

to wait for McTiernan. I needed to search for clues before darkness set in.

Jake led the way. The spot wasn't far from where we'd seen the dead cow on the Givings spread. Whoever had killed our steer must have figured that the area afforded an easy getaway.

"It's up yonder, boss," said Jake, motioning about fifty yards ahead toward a growth of cacti and some mesquite. "If there hadn't been another steer bawling its fool head off up the way, we might not have seen it. The scavengers hadn't arrived yet."

Lack of scavengers indicated that the kill had been fresh and the killer had left the scene shortly before Jake and Jimmy arrived.

We dismounted, partly because our horses were a tad put off by the lingering smell of death and partly so the scene wasn't corrupted with hoofprints.

"Hang here with the horses, Jake." I didn't need another set of boot prints, if there were any to be found. The site had already been messed up when they recovered the carcass to butcher it. I began walking toward the spot where the steer had been killed, scanning the ground for evidence with each step. I finally reached the place. Dried blood seemed to be everywhere. The killer had delivered a nasty gash into the poor beast. The steer likely bled out right quickly, so suffering would have been minimal. The slaughterhouse was actually more humane.

There were plenty of hoofprints about. There were the prints from the steer, of course. The hoofprints from the horse looked to be no different from those found at the scene of the Givings cow killing. Despite my best efforts, I found no other clues. I'd hoped the killer might have dismounted. No such luck. Whatever his reasons for killing beeves, he was careful. I headed back to Jake. "Nothing," I said dejectedly. As usual, these sorts of situations demanded patience. Lawbreakers inevitably slipped up. The sooner the better in this case.

"Guess we'll come back here later with Sheriff McTiernan," said Jake with a knowing smile.

I chuckled. "He's got to make a show of doing his duty, Jake. More importantly will be his getting the word out so other ranchers are on guard." I took a final look at the site, and we mounted up. The ride home was slow and quiet. There really wasn't much to say.

As I mounted up, my eye caught something white in the grass. "What's that?" I asked, mostly to myself.

"Looks like a playing card, boss," Jake observed. "King of Hearts."

I shrugged. "Guess somebody's not playing with a full deck." I managed a touch of humor. I had no reason to view it as any sort of evidence. The winds might have blown it from miles away.

Jake dismounted and fetched the card. He examined it closer. "Reverse side's strange, boss," continued Jake. "It depicts four horsemen."

"May I see?" I asked. Jake handed it up, and I took a gander. There were four horsemen on the back of the card all right, they represented the Apocalypse. I felt an involuntary chill. "Think I'll hang on to this," I said and stuffed it in my pocket. "I'll show it to McTiernan later," I added, knowing full well that it would tell the sheriff that I'd already investigated the site. It really was no matter, given that we'd already despoiled it.

☆☆

I guided Sheriff McTiernan to the scene a couple of hours later. By the time we finished examining the site to his satisfaction, the sun was well on its way to sinking beneath the western horizon. "Care for some dinner, Sheriff?" I asked.

"Much obliged, Junior, but I'm expected in Nuecestown," he responded.

"Perhaps another time. Please do get the word out to the local ranchers."

"Yep. I'll tell Jim Wells and Stephen Powers, too," he assured me. "Oh, and Archie Parr. Did I forget anyone?"

"I think you've mentioned those who'll be most helpful getting the word out. Do warn them about the dark-clothed rider on the gray horse."

McTiernan nodded. "You said you weren't certain about the rider, Junior. I'm not so sure we want to bias anyone without a definitive sighting."

"Thanks, Sheriff," I said perfunctorily. McTiernan seemed to have covered his political bases. I doubted he'd act quickly enough to head off any rancher vigilantism if the killings truly got out of hand. "Oh, there was this," I said and reached into my pocket. "We found this playing card near the scene. It might be something random simply blown on the wind." I handed it to him for inspection.

"Custom deck," he observed. "Sort of creepy design."

"They call them the *Four Horsemen of the Apocalypse*," I said, not knowing whether McTiernan was familiar with the Bible.

The sheriff nodded and handed it back to me. "Won't do you much good without the rest of the deck, Junior," he said with a wry grin.

"Might be a calling card; a sort of signature," I responded. "My dad told me of a man who killed priests and left a gold coin behind. Seems the men of the cloth had taken advantage of the man's sister, turning her to prostitution. The coin was symbolic of a refund of payment for services. It was the killer's signature."

McTiernan nodded. "Maybe so," he admitted, as he mounted up.

As I watched McTiernan ride off, I got to wondering at the motivation of someone who would kill cattle for no obvious purpose other than for the sake of killing. Finding the perpetrator would be like finding the proverbial needle in a haystack. South Texas, characterized as the Nueces Strip, was a vast expanse. A person could travel for days and never see a soul. In fact, they'd likely see far more beeves than people.

# FIVE
# NO ANSWERS

I SAT in my customary chair on the gallery with my feet propped up on the railing. The top runner still bore the spur gouges from my dad. Mine just added to his. So far, we hadn't a clue as to who was responsible for the killings. Cassie handled a call from Jim Wells himself over in Jim Wells County. He just wanted to let us know that he'd heard from McTiernan. There'd been no killings reported in his jurisdiction.

We managed to get our tagging and castrating chores completed. All seemed normal. In a couple of months, we'd be sending a couple of hundred head to market.

Amid all the hubbub over cattle killings, I did manage to cogitate on the offer to go undercover in the Rio Grande Valley. It was tempting but a nonstarter, as I was committed to Heaven's Gate Ranch…for now. Cassie would be upset were she to know that I'd even considered it.

I stared off into the distance. The breeze carrying aromas of the prairie gave me a certain peace. The fires in my lawman brain were burning hot. What would cause someone to do something so heinous as to kill cattle and leave the carcasses to rot? What would be their purpose? It seemed so perverse. Then it struck me like a bolt of lightning. The killer was sending a message. My first guess: he didn't like cattle? No. More likely, he didn't care for folks eating meat. Cassie had mentioned the apocalypse sort of tongue in cheek, but was this perpetrator mimicking the fourth horseman? Could be. Still, there were lots of questions but no answers. Yet, this was all beginning to come together. I was evolving a theory.

Despite telephones, the telegraph, and newspapers, communications were painfully slow. More beeves might have been killed for all we knew, and it could be weeks before we heard about them. It was frustrating to say the least.

Someone out there had seen a dark-clad rider on a gray horse.

"Hope you found it grub tasty," the barkeep said, as he retrieved the dirty plates from the table. He'd thought the stranger to be weird from the start, when the man refused the delicious steak special. He glanced out the window. "What's that thing hanging from your horse?"

The dark figure slowly looked up from his Solitaire game, then looked down and snapped another card on the stack. "Just a farm implement," he finally responded.

The barkeep was encouraged that he had actually received an answer to a question. The saloon was nearly empty, but he wasn't sure whether he should press his luck. "It's a nasty-looking farm implement," he observed.

"You ask too damned many questions," groused the card player. He snapped a king on the deck. He'd won the game.

"Enough with the damned card snapping," griped one of the two men sitting at a nearby table.

The man gave them a nasty glare, gathered the cards, and stuffed them in a pocket. He cast a soul-penetrating look at the barkeep and then at the man who'd complained. "Meal was passing fair," he growled toward the barkeep, as he stood with eyebrows knitted. He was a tall man and quite slender in the hips, but with broad, well-muscled shoulders and arms. A black beard and mustache made his entire countenance seem dark, even sinister. The black clothes enhanced the image of evil darkness.

The barkeep watched him move with a surprisingly easy gait from the saloon and climb aboard the gray horse. He shook his head. "Takes all kinds," he muttered under his breath.

"Good riddance," growled the annoyed customer.

"Damned scary scythe, if you ask me," observed another.

"What's a man carry one of them things around for anyhow?" asked still another patron.

I'd just ridden in with Pedro from checking beeves on our south pastures, as Sheriff McTiernan came riding toward us. His horse was moving at a fast walk, so I reckoned something important was on the sheriff's mind. McTiernan was never one to overstress his horse.

"Howdy, Junior. I was heading back from Nuecestown and figured to share the news in person."

"What news do you have, Sheriff?" I asked.

Pedro sat his saddle silently. He recognized from the tone of my voice that I wasn't a huge fan of McTiernan's tendency to be constantly politicking.

"Governor Culberson's office is saying there have been better than a dozen cattle killings reported in Texas, just like what happened to you and Givings."

"What's he doing about it?" I queried. It's one thing to know that others had suffered the same as us, but another to be doing something about it.

McTiernan gave me a blank look and shrugged. "Don't know. They didn't say."

I shook my head dismayingly. "Damn, John! You might as well be telling me cattle have horns."

"Well, I only know what I've been told, Junior," said McTiernan defensively. "When I learn more, I'll pass it along." With that, he turned his horse and rode off.

"Do cattle have horns?" asked Pedro with a laugh.

I couldn't help but laugh at his humor. I climbed from my saddle. "There's got to be an answer to this short of me joining the Texas Rangers again."

"We figure it out, Señor Dunn," said Pedro confidently.

"Humph!" I snorted. "I'm ready for a thick, juicy steak."

☆☆

The seemingly random killings drove me to distraction. Poor Cassie bore the brunt of my grousing.

"I'm going to Nuecestown today," I announced at breakfast.

Cassie gave me *the look* as she stood cooking eggs and bacon with two boys at her heels and a baby daughter hanging on a breast. "You have business there?" Her look suggested that I was escaping.

I poured myself some coffee and paused a second. I parked the coffee on the table and swept Sean off his feet. It was one less child hanging on Cassie. "I need some nails from Noake's store and figured to check at the inn."

"You're looking to ask about the cattle killer," Cassie observed, knowing how my lawman mind worked. She set aside the frying pan, detached Carolyn, and laid her in her cradle. "I know you can't let it go, Lucas."

"It's just that no one seems to be doing anything about it." I sipped my coffee while bouncing Sean on my knee. Naturally, I spilled a little. "Somebody must have seen something," I mused.

"What about that playing card that you found?" She knew it gave credence to her apocalyptic theory.

"Maybe other cards have been found," I mused.

Cassie placed two plates heaped with eggs and bacon before us and sat opposite me with Bode still at her heels. She took a bite of eggs, then realized I was staring at her. "What are you looking at?"

"You're beautiful," I said with loving admiration written across my face. There she stood, carrying on a conversation about something she wasn't enthusiastic about while cooking up breakfast and juggling our children. She was damned impressive…and beautiful. Now, I was messing with her reasoned thinking about the cattle killer.

I got a disconcerted look. "What do you think that's going to get you, Lucas Dunn?" She was unable to suppress a smile.

"What do you think?" I said, inferring the obvious.

Baby Carolyn was asleep, and the boys had settled into playing off in a corner.

Cassie nodded toward the upstairs.

"Nuecestown can wait," I whispered. Amazing how a few sweet words can shift a situation. I followed my giggling wife up the stairs. In a heartbeat, we got near naked and began fulfilling our most intimate passions. There was something about sexual craving that tantalized the very soul. It made our precipitous, even indiscreet, tryst all the more romantic. There'd been no romancing leading up to our seemingly illicit coupling. Perhaps, it was the risk of being discovered by a curious three-year-old that made it tantalizingly wonderful.

We lay in our afterglow.

My hand gently followed the curves of her naked body. "Yes. You are beautiful."

"Mommeee!" a voice from below demanded.

Cassie rolled on top of me. Her soft lips joined mine with the very deepest passion. She sighed, rolled from me, and grabbed her dress. "More after Nuecestown," she said breathlessly and slipped into her dress. "Darn, but you are all man, Lucas Dunn."

I sat up. If I ever smoked, I likely would have. No woman could begin to do what Cassie McCully Dunn could do for me.

I cleaned up as best I could, dressed, and headed downstairs. I gave Cassie a hug and kiss, hugged the boys, looked in at a napping Carolyn, and headed to the barn.

# SIX
# MORE KILLINGS

NUECESTOWN WAS ONLY a couple of hours ride from our ranch. It was a gorgeous day, and I found my thinking about dead cattle considerably muted after the morning's activities. Cassie was one loving woman, and our passions were mutual.

I stopped at Bert Givings' place but learned that he had already headed to Nuecestown. I reckoned I'd run into him at the old Stagecoach Inn. I thanked his wife and turned Tornado up the road.

It was a right pretty morning, and I was in no particular hurry. The buzzing bees and chirping birds lent song to the landscape. An owl hooted somewhere off in the distance. The relaxing melodies helped me enjoy the rarity of relaxation. I reminded myself that this was nature's entertainment. My dad had often ridden long distances and wiled away the loneliness of the trail by singing and simply enjoying the sounds around him. Of course, he always found himself sensitive to lurking dangers, so relaxation was a tad more difficult.

I soon found myself riding up the main street of Nuecestown. The town had been founded by Colonel Henry Kinney nearly fifty years ago and featured a ferry service across the Nueces River that facilitated the travel of folks from Corpus Christi northward. It had the largest schoolhouse pretty much anywhere around. It housed thirty-two students! A good deal of the surrounding land had been settled by my Dunn cousins from County Kildare back in Ireland. In fact, the first of my cousins to settle here had cared for Colonel Kinney's fighting cocks and served as a sutler to General Taylor during the Mexican-American War.

The town had been the scene of many a gun battle involving my dad, though they weren't the conjured-up fast-draw shoot-outs depicted in dime-store books. The town had become noted as associated with the Good Friday Raid of 1875, in which a posse led by Red John Dunn freed hostages held by Mexican bandits. The future of the town likely lay with it successfully luring a railroad to plant a depot in its midst.

I reined in at the Stagecoach Inn. There were several horses hitched out front, so I reckoned a few folks had decided to gather early.

I hitched Tornado and strode through swinging doors into the saloon portion of the inn. The bar with its polished top stretched along most of one side of the room, and four tables filled the remaining space. Sawdust covered the floor to absorb blood, sweat, booze, and foul debris. Aromas from the inn's past permeated the very woodwork. In the dim light of the room with its close quarters, the buzz of conversation was deafening.

Keep in mind that saloons out here in the west were more than about downing a few drinks. They were a sort of forum, generally offering a font of information to anyone with the inclination to listen. A patron could learn of weather predictions, Indian hostilities, the latest news from the state capitol, or who was doing what to whom. Men gathered to conduct business more in saloons than most anywhere else. Also, this establishment in Nuecestown didn't have the full amenities of saloons in the cities that could afford to feature entertainment, including pretty ladies aiming to pleasure patrons.

After adjusting my eyes, I spotted Bert Givings sitting at a rear table and talking animatedly with a couple of men. I walked on over. "Howdy, Bert," I ventured by way of interrupting.

"Oh...Junior. Good to see you. Grab a seat." He signaled to the barkeep for another round.

I was never a drinker, and a morning beer seemed unappetizing. "I'll take a coffee," I said to the barkeeper, as he served the others. I turned back to Givings. "I stopped by your spread, but your wife said you'd be here. I was coming to Nuecestown anyway."

"Well, glad you're here. Maybe your Texas Ranger know-how might help. I've been railing at John and Colt here about my cow that was killed. Seems there's been more beeves killed around these parts."

"I lost one of mine, Bert. Whatever weapon the killer used, it was a devastating blow. I examined the scene for clues as best I could. Even had McTiernan come out. He didn't find anything either."

"I did find this," offered Colt. He waved a playing card at me.

My eyes reflexively widened.

"That mean something, Junior?" asked Givings, catching my reaction.

"Don't know. We found a similar card not far from the steer that was killed at my place. We didn't think much of anything of it at the time." I found it intriguing how some perpetrators left something symbolic behind. In this case, it was beginning to look to be a sort of perpetrator calling card. I recalled the story I'd shared with McTiernan about my dad telling me about a man who killed priests and left a coin behind. In the case of this cattle killer, it was sending a message to the world that he had killed the animal and no one else.

"Whatcha reckon can be done?" asked John as he took a long sip of beer.

I wondered how much I should tell. If I mentioned the rider on the gray horse, anyone riding such a steed might be endangered by a vigilante mentality. "It occurs to me that the only way we'll find this sort of man is to catch him in the act. That's how they used to catch hiders."

There were nods of agreement.

"If y'all hear of any further killings, please let me know." I found myself succumbing to my lawman inclinations. Nothing like a good mystery to kindle my fire. As I took a sip of coffee, I overheard an animated conversation behind me.

☆☆

*"Madre de Dios!"* exclaimed a man of obvious Mexican descent, gesticulating wildly with his hands. *"El presidente es un tonto."*

"Ah, Carlos. *Relajar. No puedes hacer nada.*" The man told Carlos that there was nothing he could do.

*"Díaz es un idiota,"* insisted Carlos.

They gripped my attention. I half listened to the lingering conversation about cattle with Bert, John, and Colt while keeping an ear attentive to the talk behind me. Apparently, Mexican President Diaz was stirring up some sort of problem. That it reached so far as Nuecestown was a concern. If I'd accepted Lieutenant Smith's offer, I'd quite possibly be dealing with whatever they were discussing. I yearned to learn more, as I tried to stay politely involved in the conversation about cattle.

*"Díaz paga a los rebeldes,"* postulated Carlos, hitting the table for emphasis.

That got my attention. President Diaz was paying rebels. I speculated as to whether it was a ploy on the part of Mexico's president to distract serious political opponents. I wondered whether Captain Hughes knew about this. For now, it was none of my business. I had a ranch to worry about, and now a mysterious cattle killer with some strange apocalyptic connection.

"Hey, *gringo*!" said one of the Mexicans. *"Me oyes*?" He accused me of listening in.

Well, they were talking loudly enough that their conversation was hard to miss. Suddenly, their talk had become my business. *"Lo siento. No pude evitarlo,"* I told them that I was sorry but couldn't help it.

*"Gringos muy malo,"* accused Carlos.

*"Tranquilo, amigo,"* I cautioned the Mexicans to ease up. I didn't see cause for any bad feelings. The Mexicans often did have a tough go of it in Texas. They held resentments from better than half a century back, while a lot of Texans chose to treat them as second-class citizens.

Givings and the others went silent as they saw tensions brewing.

No one saw my hand slip to my holster. I slowly slid my revolver out as a precaution.

The man behind Carlos stood and laid a hate-filled gaze on me. His hand suddenly grasped the butt of his gun.

Before he could think about drawing it, he was looking into the muzzle of my Smith & Wesson. *"Basta*!" I warned. "Enough!" I repeated in English. "Y'all can talk of the Mexican president and his problems all you want, but don't be bringing those problems here. Y'all are Americans now."

Carlos nodded, while the man behind him sat as though he were a deflated balloon. "You are right, Señor Dunn," he said with a smile.

"What do you think?" asked Givings.

His question brought my attention back to my tablemates. "About what?" I blurted, revealing that I'd not been paying attention. I gave an apologetic look around the table.

"You listenin' in on them greasers," laughed Colt.

They'd caught me. "Sorry. It's the Texas Ranger in me. There's trouble in Mexico."

Colt laughed. "There'll always be trouble in Mexico. That one greaser was looking to pull on you."

I shrugged. I didn't reckon to argue, much less deal with derogatory name-calling. "Now, what did you ask?" I said, turning to Givings.

"We got to make sure all our hands are gathering what they can about this damned cattle killer."

"Makes perfect sense," I added. "Put some heat on Sheriff McTiernan, too. And the other sheriffs."

"I wonder where the killer is from and where he hangs out?" interjected John.

"Putting the word out to saloons and hotels wouldn't hurt, except we don't know what we're looking for," I advised. "What's the perpetrator look like? Anybody know?" These were rhetorical questions, as the answers were obvious. I knew that the whole mess had my hackles up.

Sheriff McTiernan strode into the saloon. He took one

look at our little gathering and walked on over with a grim expression. "Been another one, boys. Ranch just east of the King Ranch. Steer got sliced up pretty bad and left to rot like the others."

"Anything stand out, Sheriff?" I asked.

"One of the ranch hands found a playing card caught in some grass near the kill," replied McTiernan.

"Humph!" I exclaimed. "Whoever's killing our beeves has a calling card, so to speak. That's the third instance of a card being found at the site. The man disappears like a ghost."

Givings shrugged. "So, our killer plays cards. That narrows it down," he said sarcastically.

"Somebody out there will eventually see the killer at the scene," I postulated. "When that happens, we've got to spread the word right quickly." I knew it was a vast landscape, and a reasonably careful perpetrator could easily operate unseen.

"I agree, Junior," said McTiernan. "I've reached out to other sheriffs, but no word yet. Oh, and I've seen one of those cards. There was the king of spades on one side and the Four Horsemen of the Apocalypse on the reverse side. Strange deck. Never seen one like it."

Apocalypse? That grabbed my attention. Cassie's suggestion was grabbing hold of my thinking on the challenge we were facing. "I appreciate what we're up against, gentlemen. I share your anger and frustration." With that, I got up and headed out to the general store.

Carlos and his Mexican companions nodded at me as I strode by. They might not have liked me, but they surely respected me.

☆☆

Meanwhile, Mexican President Diaz was cooking up a morass of economic trouble in the sense that US investment interests were strong despite a hostile climate. Rebellious factions in Mexico came and went seemingly as frequently as the sun rose and set. The Spanish-American War had established the US as the leading power in the western hemisphere, and Diaz was none too happy about it. His hold on Mexico was seen as tenuous at best.

The economic instability made for political as well as economic instability along the Rio Grande. Texas Ranger Captain Hughes had his hands full. It was no surprise when I received a letter almost begging me to come south and help root out trouble along the border.

Once again, I turned down the offer. It was tempting, but I found myself determined to solve the mysterious killing of our cattle. International political squabbles would have to wait. As a matter of fact, I wasn't so sure I'd want to deal with persuading Cassie to let me put on the Texas Ranger badge again.

I joined McTiernan over at the Nuecestown jail. I appreciated that his visit saved me a trip to see him in Corpus Christi. Not that it wasn't an easy enough ride, but I appreciated the convenience and the fact that I didn't feel obligated to spend time with my cousins living along the road to the city.

I pulled up a chair opposite the sheriff. "Dang, John, this place gets more run-down every time I stop by. Any prisoner might fear for the roof caving in on his head."

McTiernan eased back in his big chair behind the desk and calmly lit a cigar. He chuckled at my humor. Sometimes reality is the funniest joke of all. "Tell the folks around here to pay up their taxes and we'll get a new roof. Of course, it may make no difference. I hear Uriah Lott reckons to skirt this place with the railroad he's planning. Could turn Nuecestown into a ghost town."

"I must admit that railroads have changed the economic landscape," I said with conviction.

He nodded. "Pretty much. I heard that you turned down an offer from Captain Hughes. Reckon you're set on hunting down this character that's killing beeves?" he observed.

"Guess that's clear as daylight," I responded. "You have any thoughts beyond what we talked about at the inn?"

McTiernan shook his head. "Your guess is as good as mine, Junior."

Ambrose McTavish sat quietly in his saddle, watching the morning mist embrace the dozen beeves grazing before him. The brim of his black hat dipped low enough to nearly cover his dark eyes, while his black cape fully enshrouded him atop the pale horse. "Aye, thar's a fat one," he growled. "Good as any we be seein'." He pushed his cape back to free his arms and untied the thong that held the scythe in place. This was no ordinary tool. He'd designed it special to suit his task. He unfolded the big blade from the long wooden snath with its grip and locked it in place. He tested the edge. It was razor-sharp. He ran a whetstone over the blade edge just to be sure of its sharpness. This scythe wouldn't be cutting grass.

The crowning touch was a mask. If he was going to be the Grim Reaper, he felt the need to look the part. The ghoulish white mask he slipped over his face completed the image of the Pale Rider of the Apocalypse. He was about to deliver death.

He eased his pale steed gentle-like alongside the steer he'd selected. "You'll hardly feel a thing," he assured the beast. With that, he raised the scythe high overhead. He brought it down with an explosive grunt and force generated by his massive shoulders. The blade cut deep through the steer's chest, splitting its heart in two. The beast grunted, tried to bawl, and dropped to its knees before keeling over. In seconds, the steer had bled out.

McTavish sat high in his saddle high and looked around. There was still no one to be seen. The surrounding mist had been great cover. The other beeves grazed peacefully as though nothing had happened. He wiped the blade clean before folding and securing it. He reached into his brocaded black vest, flipped a playing card, and watched it flutter to the ground near the slaughtered steer.

"Shame I must sacrifice a few of you to save the others," he lamented to the dead steer by way of confession. He then turned the gray and lost himself in the mist. "How many was that?" he whispered to himself rhetorically. He wondered how many he must kill before they stopped breeding cattle. The only emotion he knew was a passion against meat. Raw, roasted, fried…it was no matter. Elder Barnabas had assured him that only then would the world be saved from oblivion.

McTavish was convinced that eating meat spelled apocalypse; the very end of the world. He was out to save mankind from this fate. He didn't for a minute think of himself as evil. It would have shocked him to think anyone might do so. That would be pure nonsense. Likewise, some might think him insane. They were the crazy ones who ate meat and would perish at the world's end. His sense of being absolutely right in his purpose was embedded in his brain like wagon ruts in the limestone of western trails. "When I'm done, they won't be raising cattle anymore," he said reassuringly to his horse. He was committed to killing as many as he could.

A drink and playing a bit of Solitaire sounded good to him about now as he bided his time until his next message.

## SEVEN
# VIGILANTE?

UPON ENTERING OUR HOME, I was immediately accosted by Sean and Bode. I managed to hang my hat and gun belt while tossing my saddlebags in a corner. With Bode in one arm and Sean tailing behind, I headed to the kitchen and Cassie.

"I received a surprise telephone call this afternoon," said Cassie upon my arriving home from Nuecestown.

"Oh?" I queried.

"Are you acquainted with Robert Kleberg?" she asked with a knowing smile. Didn't everybody know Robert Kleberg, the man Richard King entrusted with his huge ranch?

"He called?" I asked incredulously.

Cassie nodded as she busied herself at the stove.

"So, are you going to tell me what his call was about?" Cassie had a certain teasing way when she had some juicy information that I was unaware of. I sidled over to her, took out my Bowie knife, and began peeling potatoes.

"Put that thing away, you ruffian," she teased. "He suggested that you call Archer Parr about the cattle trouble.

He said to tell you that the King Ranch wasn't interested in hiring the Pinkertons...whatever that's supposed to mean."

I knew that this meant that Kleberg was looking to keep a low profile. I caught on right quickly that he was looking to hire a private sleuth to solve a problem that was growing bigger every day. Better than a dozen cattle had now been slain. As yet, not a soul had seen whoever was killing them, though I still held to that brief glimpse of someone near the scene of the killing of Givings' steer. "You know what this means?"

"Not Texas Ranger work," she said by way of reminding me of my promise.

"You know these cattle killings impact us as well as all of our neighbors. I'll bet that Kleberg is looking to hire me to be a private detective, but paying for it through Parr. It's not Texas Ranger work, but it's similar. Likely pays a lot better." I poured us some coffee, while Cassie finished cooking dinner. It gave her time to think.

"Would you be in any danger?" she ventured.

"I think we're dealing with someone with some sort of axe to grind against ranchers. If he's as nutty as his actions thus far, there could be some danger." I tried to be honest. It was always best to be that way up front, because she had a way of eventually getting to truths. Besides, there was no love between husband and wife without truth. I might not know the outcome from expressing a truth, but I knew the outcome were I not to share it honestly.

Cassie began dishing out dinner. She banged the spatula against the pan as was her habit when she felt out of sorts. She could hardly be blamed for wanting me to stay safe. "They always turn to a Lucas Dunn, don't they?" she asked resignedly.

Being a Dunn was a mixed bag. Cassie was right, and

there were both fear and pride in her question. I waited silently until she had fully served up dinner.

"Let me get the lay of the land from Parr before we start worrying about what I am or am not going to do. I won't be a lawman, so can't make any arrest. Best case would be tracking the cattle killer down." I shoved a juicy slice of steak into my mouth. Damn, but it was good. I not only married the prettiest girl, but a great cook, too.

She watched me enjoy that delicious morsel of beef and smiled. "I know you'll make the right decision, Lucas." She gave me that look; the one that she knew lit my fire. I glanced at Shawn and Bode. They were yawning in between bites of potatoes and steak, sliced thin for them.

I finally got around to savoring a slice of cherry pie while I watched the boys finish dinner. "I'll clean the dishes while you put the boys to bed," I volunteered with a knowing smile.

I can say that those dishes and the cooking utensils were sparkling clean by the time Cassie had the boys cleaned up and in bed.

She found a bottle of wine and set it on the table for me to open and bring upstairs with a couple of crystal glasses. She gave an over-the-shoulder *come-hither* look as she headed up the stairs.

I dried the last cooking pot, grabbed the wine and glasses, and headed upstairs to her waiting arms. I must say that ranching here at Heaven's Gate with my family was vastly superior to running around as a Texas Ranger. The perquisites were certainly wonderful.

I called Archer Parr, but he was away from his office. I learned that he'd be around in the early afternoon, so reckoned to take a chance on catching up to him. I saddled Tornado and headed for San Diego over in Duval County.

I took my time, as my rides on Tornado had grown ever fewer with my having given up the badge. Most of my riding was confined to the considerable acres of our ranch. I had begun hearing stories of what some folks referred to as a horseless carriage. It was being called the automobile. Somebody named Benz had apparently invented the vehicle. The Corpus Christi Caller Times reported that a Colonel Green, owner of the Texas Midland Railroad, had purchased a gasoline-powered automobile. The newspaper called it a St. Louis Phaeton-Runabout. I'd heard that the contraptions were downright expensive. Green lived in Terrell, about a stone's throw from Dallas and not far from the Corsicana oilfields.

I thought back on my run-in with the Irish Mob and how they'd planned to wrestle the Railroad Commission of Texas for control over the oil business. It didn't take a mental giant to figure that the days of traveling on horseback were numbered. Eventually, automobiles would become so numerous as to become affordable for many folks. It might be a few years off, but I'd bet my spurs it would happen. I patted Tornado's neck, as much reassuring myself as him that I'd be riding him for a while yet.

While I was fascinated by the concept of the automobile and how it would change our lives as surely as the railroads and telephones, my thoughts drifted to the cattle killer. Maybe Cassie wasn't so far off with her comparison to the biblical pale rider of the apocalypse. Whoever this man was, he seemed to hold some hate-filled passions over cattle. I'd already figured him for a nutcase.

I reckoned that my conversation with Parr would involve him engaging me on behalf of Kleberg to hunt down—or, rather, identify—the cattle killer. This would keep Kleberg's hands clean. It was little wonder that he didn't want the Pinkertons involved, as that might have splashed the killings over every newspaper in America. For now, we wanted any publicity to stay local. We'd not as yet heard of killings outside of South Texas.

Soon, I found myself in San Diego, sitting astride Tornado before Archer Parr's office. There was activity inside, so he was apparently there. I didn't feature riding all the way out to his ranch in Benevides, so appreciated a rest from the saddle. He'd been reelected as Duval County Commissioner, and some were beginning to call him the Duke of Duval owing to his growing political power. I chuckled at the title, as my cousin Patrick Dunn ranched the northern seventy-five miles of Padre Island outside of Corpus Christi and had taken the moniker Duke of Padre Island. Shoot, I didn't reckon to be duke of anything.

I climbed from my saddle, hitched Tornado, and headed for the front door to Parr's office. I didn't bother to knock, as it was technically public property. I swung the door open and found myself in a large room that doubled as a foyer and secretarial space. It was a modest affair, but I reckoned it would get fancier along with Parr's ambition.

By pure chance, I nearly knocked Parr over as I entered. He'd been posting some announcement on a bulletin board beside the doorway and hadn't heard my boots clomp on the boardwalk outside. He recoiled, then laughed. "Well, I'll be. I heard you might be showing up, Junior." He shook my hand vigorously and motioned me to his office.

"Good to see you again, Archer."

He ushered me into his office, told his clerk to leave us undisturbed, and closed the office door behind us. "Have a seat, Junior." He was about to sit, but paused. "Oh, pardon me. Care for some coffee?"

I nodded as I sat.

With that, he strode over and poured two cups of coffee. "Guess Bob Kleberg's reached out to you," he noted.

I nodded again.

He placed a cup of coffee in front of me. "Seems we have a serious problem that needs solving without raising too much of a ruckus. You've earned yourself a reputation for solving tough cases that'd do your dad proud."

I tried not to blush at the compliment. After all, I was being buttered up for something. "Why not the Pinkertons or the Texas Rangers?" I asked, knowing the answer.

"I admire the Rangers, Junior, but we're looking to eliminate the problem, not take it to court." He smiled. "As to the Pinkertons, we don't need national press." Parr sat behind his desk, took a sip of coffee, and broke out a cigar. "Care for a cigar?" He knew the answer but was being polite.

I couldn't miss the word *eliminate*. "I'm no hired gun, Archer, and surely no vigilante," I advised solemnly.

"I didn't mean that sort of elimination, Junior. Lord knows, we don't want blood on our hands." He rolled his eyes as he put a match to the cigar.

Or, my hands. I couldn't help but figure that his assurance was ringing hollow.

"No matter the outcome, you couldn't earn in a year at Heaven's Gate Ranch what you'll earn helping us." He smiled broadly and flashed his fingers…once…twice…eight more times just for show. "Plus expenses," he added. He was offering ten thousand dollars. That was serious money in South Texas in 1900.

I reflexively gulped, a reaction that Parr couldn't have missed. The offer was tempting. "You say I'm not to eliminate the problem?" I sought reassurance. We both knew what *eliminate* meant.

"Just find him. We'll take care of the rest," he said with

open palm raised as though pledging. "You'll get half the fee up front. Keep it whether you succeed or not."

*Fee*? This was a nice way of putting it. Five thousand dollars sure seemed attractive; generous for sure. It was several years of Texas Ranger pay and nearly a decade's worth for a cowboy. How could I refuse? I couldn't. I took a sip of coffee to try to steady myself while Parr calmly blew a smoke ring to the ceiling. I leaned back and gave him my steeliest gaze. "Okay. I'm your man, Archer. I'll give it my best effort."

Parr sent two more smoke rings aloft. "Thanks kindly, Junior. We're confident that you're up to the job."

That was obvious, or I wouldn't have been sitting there.

"You still banking at Corpus Christi National Bank?" inquired Parr.

"Yes, sir." I happily responded.

"Your down payment will be sitting in your account tomorrow. Good luck, Junior. We're counting on you." Parr ruffled some papers to signify that our meeting was over, then politely ushered me to the door. We shook hands. Already deep in thought as to my task, I found myself in a sort of shock and staring at Tornado. He broke my trance with a whinny.

Well, I was five thousand dollars wealthier, but as yet had no new ideas as to how to catch the cattle killer. As I departed Parr's office, I got to thinking that the term *cattle killer* didn't do justice to this nefarious pervert. Bovine butcher? Stock slayer? Dogie butcher? I suppose it wasn't especially catchy to say that my task was to pursue a cattle killer, he was more like an assassin. It wasn't just about killing. Whoever the perpetrator was, he was more than simply a killer. Crazed as it seemed, he had a purpose, a message he was trying to deliver. I fancied referring to him as the *cattle assassin*.

I was now being paid to catch this cattle assassin, this crazed killer of beeves who had dubbed himself some sort of apocalyptic savior of the world. Actually, it was more than that. As a rancher, I had a personal stake in this. Combined with my lawman heritage, it brought me a sense of duty to my family and fellow Texans. The economics aside, duty was critically important to me and should be to most anyone. Folks living together needed to follow rules. There were God's rules and man's rules.

The law establishes and enforces the rules. Without laws, every man would become his own fortress against lawbreakers. Vigilantism would flourish, especially as one man's law differed from another's. Yet, there always seems to be those who test the law, who are determined to break it for whatever purpose they hang to. If it were not for those who can't or won't ride a straight trail, folks like me would be unneeded.

Now, I pointed Tornado toward Heaven's Gate Ranch and gave him his head. I was anxious to share the news with Cassie. I reminded myself that this was Texas. It was part of a western frontier that had yet to be tamed and perhaps never would. The soil took as much as it gave. It demanded total respect.

There were folks out there like the cattle killer who had personal agendas they'd carry out—right or wrong—with utter disregard for any collateral damage. Folks seemed bent on striving for some perfection they called utopia. My dad told me about a fellow named Sir Thomas More who wrote a book about this mythical place he called Utopia, which was defined as a place of ideal perfection, especially in laws, government, and social conditions. After my dad described it, he was pleased with my reaction. I asked whose utopia this was, mine, his, God's, the government's, some stranger's? I expect I was holding an accurate perspective on the concept of perfection. Dad said that was good, because the only perfection he knew of was the heaven described in the Holy Bible. That was good enough for me. Now, I had to figure what sort of utopian myth the cattle assassin was working toward.

☆☆

I dismounted in front of our barn and led Tornado to his stall, taking my time currying and sweet-talking him just like most any cowboy might. I began to hum a little ditty. I couldn't sing a lick, but Tornado tolerated me.

"You coming to dinner or just going to serenade that horse?" asked Cassie.

I spun around with a sheepish grin and swept her up into my arms. "Whatcha serving?"

She gave me a wink. "It depends."

"I've been hired to track down the cattle assassin. I just need to identify him. No badge, no arrest." I gave her one of those looks that said there was more.

"And?" she asked, as she pressed herself a tad seductively against me.

"Ten thousand dollars," I blurted and planted a kiss that fully devoured her lips.

Cassie pushed me back into the hay but didn't follow. She stood with arms on her hips and chest heaving with unmet desire. "Later, cowboy. Kids are waiting for chow."

I got up and picked straw from myself, as I followed her like a stallion chasing a mare in heat to the house and dinner. Cassie was easy to follow, as she had a naturally sexy sway—not overdone, mind you—to her hips as she walked. I sure looked forward to later.

# EIGHT
# DETECTIVE WORK

SO, here I was with some heavy-duty detective work ahead of me. This would mean visiting the watering holes around the countryside where folks—mostly men—gathered to talk, drink, play cards, and often conduct business. I didn't fancy myself a drinker other than an occasional beer or glass of wine, so saloons were mostly alien to me. Nevertheless, one did what one had to do.

This fine, sweltering, hot August morning found me plodding gently along atop Tornado. After all, he was feeling the heat, too. I suppose the good news was that I'd be gone a handful of days at a time. It would give me plenty of opportunities to tend to my responsibilities at Heaven's Gate Ranch while picking up any new local news or rumors about the cattle assassin. Of course, nearly everyone had an opinion of whom it might be.

I removed my hat and did my best to wipe the sweatband dry. My bandana was already soaked, so I can't say that it was especially effective. I found a shady spot and decided to give Tornado and me a break. I continued to wrestle with this cattle assassin. Where was he from? What was traipsing through his mind? It occurred to me that he was not likely very stable. That alone gave me a creepy feeling. He hadn't killed a human so far as we knew, yet that wasn't much of a relief. I couldn't help but feel a bit uneasy, as you never could tell what a person might do when someone closed in on their trail. There were intangibles that might be dealt with in a split second. In this sleuthing business, one could never be sure when death might be reaching for your reins.

So, I rode on into Beeville. I figured to begin with this town, as it was nearest to the first killings, and then work my way westward. I reckoned to spend the night there, so reined in at the stable near the Commercial Hotel. I made sure Tornado was comfortable, grabbed my saddlebags and Winchester, and headed to the hotel. It was a two-story structure at the corner of Corpus Christi and Washington Streets that was in good enough shape to be inviting. It had changed ownership several times in the past half dozen years and been damaged and repaired after the hurricane of 1886. Before entering, I took a gander up and down the streets and caught sight of Schilo's Saloon. There were a half dozen others that I'd be checking out.

My spurs jangling on the wooden floor caught the attention of the desk clerk. He scrambled to the registration desk and greeted me with a forced smile.

"Y'all have a room available for a couple of nights?" I inquired. I figured that Beeville was a big enough town that it was worth a two-night commitment.

"Yes, sir," replied the clerk. He gave me a once-over that focused on the Smith & Wesson on my hip and the Winchester in my hand. "Will the first floor do?"

"So long as it's comfortable. I've had a long day in the saddle."

The clerk spun the register around to me. "You have business in Beeville, sir?"

I felt as though it was a rather inane question, but figured the young man was just trying to make friendly small talk. "Yep. Sure do. Where can a hungry man grab some grub and drink?" I knew the answer, but reckoned to give the clerk a chance to be helpful.

"Schilo's Saloon up the street has pretty fair food, sir." He spun the register back around and took a long look at my name as though trying to recall something. "Welcome to the Commercial Hotel, Mr. Dunn." He handed me a key. "You'll be in room 102 down that hall to the right," he advised with a finger pointing in the direction of my room.

"Any chance I can get a bath?"

"Sure, Mr. Dunn. I'll get that set up for you," responded the clerk. He paused. "Er, pardon, sir. Are you the Texas Ranger who solved those murders in Kerrville?"

There was no escaping my past. "Yes," I replied with a resigned sigh.

"Well, my cousin lives there and told me about it. Great to have you visiting here in Beeville, sir." He offered a grateful sort of expression. "I'll get right on that bath, Mr. Dunn." He paused. "Are you still a Texas Ranger?"

I shook my head. "Just ranching these days, son." I went to pick up my saddlebags, but the young man had already grabbed them and was leading me to my room.

I was hungry, but reckoned I'd enjoy dinner more if I got rid of the trail dust caked to my sweat-drenched body. Blessedly, the room had one of the new electric fans. It had an especially cooling effect on a wet body.

Properly bathed and with fresh clothes, I headed to Schilo's Saloon. I reckoned to visit three saloons this night and save the other four for tomorrow. I figured to head to the Midway Saloon and Sap Saloon after dining at Schilo's. Seven saloons? Beeville was certainly a happening place. Bee County was situated pretty much at the intersecting of ranches and farms. Barbed wire hadn't missed the area, as it was divided about as much as mankind could imagine dividing vast acreages into smaller spreads.

Beeville wasn't all that far from Victoria and Linnville. Both towns had been attacked by the famed Comanche Chief Buffalo Hump sixty years ago. I made a note to myself to visit Victoria. Linnville had been destroyed by Buffalo Hump, so there was no point in heading to where it had been. No self-respecting cattle assassin would likely hang there anyhow.

There were several tables available as I strode into Schilo's Saloon. Most any other time, I'd have headed to the bar upon entering, but I was trail-weary and hungry. The hotel clerk had advised me that "Papa" Fritz Schilo fancied himself a pretty fair chef, so I looked forward to an excellent dinner to help me overcome having to miss Cassie's cooking.

I eased myself into a chair at one of the empty tables. I caught the eye of a young lady who appeared to be serving folks.

She strolled over. "Mr. Schilo is offering a steak special this evening, sir."

"Steak? That will be fine." I didn't have to say *rare*. This was Texas. No one ate meat cooked to the texture of shoe leather.

"Coffee?" she asked, knowing it was expected in Texas. There was a comfort in dining at a place that catered to patron expectations.

I nodded to her while noting that the barkeep was

keeping a wary eye on me, as he wiped glasses and placed them in a nearby rack. I figured him for the sort that prided himself in knowing what was going on around the town and would surely note anything out of the ordinary. I was tempted to walk on over and have a chat, but decided my empty stomach took priority.

Between savory morsels of steak cooked to perfection and sips of fine coffee, I kept an eye on the clientele. There were no unusual characters. The customers were mostly ranch hands or farm laborers dressed for their trades. I was probably the best-dressed in the saloon. As the evening wore on, a couple of men entered with ladies on their arms. These didn't appear to be soiled doves but rather spouses or girlfriends.

I finally decided it was time to check out the Sap and Midway Saloons, so paid my tab and gathered my Winchester. Before departing, it seemed as appropriate a time as ever to get acquainted with the barkeep. I eased on over to the bar and motioned him over.

He was a burly man with a handlebar mustache, a neck that rivaled an ox, and well-muscled arms. He didn't appear to be the type a person with any sense would pick a fight with. The barkeep generally stood with those huge arms crossed over his barrel chest when not serving drinks. The reflection in the mirror behind the bar told me that a shotgun was parked under the bar top. I suspected he knew how to use it. Scars from shot scarred a couple of places on the floor as proof that he did. "Can I help you?" he asked with a surprisingly pleasant voice. A man of his size could certainly afford to be polite.

"Just enjoyed Mr. Schilo's fine cooking." I stated the obvious, as he was already well aware of my eating habits based on what he'd seen this evening. He likely knew whether I'd seasoned my steak and how many bites I'd taken. "Wondered whether you might answer a question of two?"

"You the law?" he asked. It was an obvious question in his business, as most any lawman worth his salt inquired with bartenders.

I smiled. "Used to be. I'm strictly a rancher these days. Own a spread out past Nuecestown."

The barkeep smiled as though accepting my answer. "What's your first question?"

"Just wondered whether you'd seen any especially unusual folks wander through in the past few weeks?"

The barkeep chuckled. "Lots of strange critters run through here, mister." He took to wiping out a shot glass. "You got a question with more bite?"

"The person I'm looking for might have been wearing black and riding a light-colored horse. That ring a bell?" I pressed hopefully.

"Ha! Now that you mention it, there was a strange gent, came through here a couple of weeks back. He was eccentric in a spooky sort of way. Kind of unnatural. He wanted nothing to do with beef. He ate strictly vegetables." The barkeep paused in thought. "Fact was, he was a bit nasty over meat, thought it was evil or something. We served him. He rode off to God knows where on a pale horse, sort of a light gray."

"Anything special about the horse?" I asked.

"Some sort of stick or lance was hanging from the saddle. I didn't ask about it."

"Any idea where this gent was spending the night?" I was overjoyed that I might have finally gotten a break in my hunt for the cattle assassin.

"Nope. He wasn't inclined toward conversation. In fact, he was what you might call grouchy. I pegged him for being from back east. Anyway, he left here and headed west," offered the barkeep. He paused, as another memory crept into his powers of recall. "He sat for a couple of hours playing Solitaire before dining. He had a way of snapping the cards that was a tad annoying."

"I'm grateful," I concluded. "I'm staying for another night at the Commercial Hotel. Let me know if anything else comes to mind." I dropped a silver dollar on the bar and departed.

Well, I had my first honest clues. What the barkeep had seen matched up with what I thought I'd seen on Givings' ranch.

I checked out the Sap and Midway Saloons, but the barkeeps hadn't seen anyone fitting the description the bartender at Schilo's Saloon had described, much less any other unusual characters. I headed back to the hotel. Come morning, I figured to do a bit of snooping around Beeville.

☆☆

Another oppressively hot day greeted me. At least, traveling around town would offer occasional respite as afforded by the shade of buildings and relative cooler temperatures inside stores.

As I was about to leave the hotel, I realized that I hadn't asked the clerk about the cattle assassin. I stopped at the registration desk and motioned him over. "Just curious," I opened. "I expect you see quite a few folks here at the hotel. Just wondered whether you might recall someone in particular."

The clerk was all ears, as he nearly ran to the desk in his eagerness. I suppose the possibility of assisting a former Texas Ranger was motivation enough.

"I'm looking for a man who dresses in black and rides a light gray horse."

The clerk's smile faded. "No one through here by that description, Mr. Dunn."

"Thanks. Let me know if you recall anything."

"You working on a case?" he asked.

I leaned toward him, put my hand aside my mouth, and whispered. "Private matter. Can't tell you." With that, I smiled and departed.

I headed to the stable. Perhaps, the stable boy had seen something. Pale gray horses were not especially common.

Turned out the stable boy had seen no such horse. Apparently, my assassin hadn't stayed very long in Beeville, certainly not long enough to take a room or stable a horse.

I reckoned there wasn't much point in continuing to hang around in Beeville, so I headed back to the hotel and checked out. The clerk was good enough to refund my advance payment for a second night.

☆☆

While my assassin was purported by the barkeep to have headed west, I sensed that he'd journeyed to Texas from the east. He just might have swung through Victoria on his way.

If Beeville was a happening place, my initial impression of Victoria was that it had a certain edge to it. It wasn't so long ago that I'd passed through Victoria via railroad on my way to tackle the Irish Mob. Matter of fact, Victoria was a vibrant railroad hub served by five railroads, including the Southern Pacific's San Antonio and Aransas Pass Railway that Uriah Lott had been forced to sell. Along with the Galveston, Harrisburg and San Antonio Railway, Lott's railroad adventure was just another that the Southern Pacific gobbled up.

I decided to begin with a visit to Sheriff George Heck. He coincidentally served as city marshal. With that obscene deposit in our bank account in Corpus Christi and expenses being covered, I reckoned to enjoy the finest hotel the city had to offer. I set my sights on the Denver Hotel, as it had earned a reputation as one of the best hotels in the nation. "Money is no object," I murmured to myself as I headed for Heck's office.

Turning Tornado up the main street, I reflected on the money. My daddy had advised me that where much is given, much is expected. It wouldn't do to let my benefactors down. I was encouraged by the clues turned up by my investigations in Beeville. The cattle assassin—or the man I assumed to be the cattle assassin—wore black, rode a pale horse, hated meat, and enjoyed playing Solitaire. Oh, and he apparently had some sort of device attached to his saddle. I got to thinking that it might be what he used to kill the cattle.

Reining in before Sheriff Heck's office, I climbed down from Tornado and hitched him to the rail. I'd never met Heck, but heard that he was a straight shooter who stuck to his knitting around Victoria. Lord knows, with all the railroads and four saloons, there was plenty to keep a lawman busy. I knocked on Heck's door.

"Yep. Come on in. Coffee's hot an' cups are empty," came a friendly voice from within.

I opened the door and stepped in. "Howdy, I'm Junior Dunn, up here visiting from Nuecestown. I'm looking for Sheriff Heck." I reached my hand across the desk to the slender, comfortable-looking man sitting behind it.

"Well, you found him. I'm city marshal, too," he added with a grin. "You the Dunn fella that's been working for Captain Hughes?" asked Heck as he shook my hand.

"I'm the one," I responded. "I'm back to ranching now,

but we've been facing a problem and wondered whether y'all have had to deal with it around here."

"Grab yourself a cup of coffee and set a spell, Mr. Dunn." Heck pointed to the coffee pot and empty cups. "Just brewed it, so it's hot."

I poured myself a cup of coffee and sat opposite Heck's desk. His was a modestly appointed office. A rack with rifles and a couple of shotguns decorated one wall, a window and the door to the street took another wall, a third was plastered with the latest wanted posters, and the other wall offered the entrance to the cell block. Cell keys hung on a nail beside the doorway. "Somebody has been killing our beeves."

Heck shook his head a bit. "That's nothing new. Hungry folk been doing that now and again for years."

"This is different, Sheriff. The perpetrator has struck a dozen ranches in South Texas, including the King Ranch. He kills a steer with some bladed weapon and leaves it to rot. And he drops a playing card as his signature."

Heck sat in stunned silence, then sighed. "Whew. I hope to hell nothing like that happens here. How are you involved, Mr. Dunn?"

"One of my beeves was killed. I've been hired privately to find the man killing the beeves." I glanced at the wanted posters on the wall, but saw nothing that caught my eye. "I've learned that the man passed through Beeville and reckoned to find out whether he'd come from this way. With all the railroads serving y'all, I thought the man might have passed through Victoria from back east."

"You know what he looks like?" asked Heck.

"Roughly. The man wears black and rides a pale horse, gray to be specific. He apparently won't eat meat. The killer passes time playing Solitaire. I understand that he snaps the cards, much to the annoyance of folks sitting near him.

A barkeep in Beeville said he speaks with an eastern accent."

"Doesn't eat meat? Damn! He sure ain't a Texan," observed Heck with a chuckle. "I'll keep an eye out for your man, Mr. Dunn, but it sounds like he's busy down in your neck of the range."

"Thanks. I'd appreciate any help." I passed along my telephone number at Heaven's Gate. "Please give a call if you see or hear anything. Sheriff McTiernan down in Corpus Christi is also looking for the killer." I stood. "If you think of anything, I'll be at the Denver Hotel."

With that, I left Heck and headed for the Denver Hotel. It had gotten late in the day, so there was no point in heading back toward Nuecestown tonight.

"May I assist you, sir?" asked the desk clerk.

"I'd be obliged to enjoy one of your rooms for tonight," I replied.

He placed the registration ledger in front of me. "Please sign in, sir. You'll be in room 210."

I scrawled my name and took the room key.

The clerk looked at my entry in the register. "Oh, Mr. Dunn. I've got a message for you from Sheriff Heck." The clerk handed me a scrap of paper.

That hadn't taken very long. I unfolded the paper. Buried inside was an article clipped from a newspaper. "Er, thanks kindly," I said to the clerk. I grabbed my saddlebags and headed for the stairway.

"The bellhop can take those, Mr. Dunn," offered the desk clerk.

I'd already slung them over my shoulder and had my Winchester in hand. "Thanks. I can handle them. If you could stable my horse—the Appaloosa out there—I'd appreciate it." I walked away, nearly tripping over a chair as I began to read the clipping. "Holy smoke!" I exclaimed too loudly.

Turns out that the clerk at the Commercial Hotel in Beeville had happened on the article in a newspaper published a month or so back and, knowing I was headed to Victoria, sent it to Sheriff Heck. It was from some eastern paper, but the name of the newspaper had been trimmed away, leaving only the city from which it had been published: Washington, DC. I understood our nation's capital to be a highly political place. I'd also heard that the famed author Mark Twain had described it in a quote: "It's filled with liars and politicians, but I repeat myself." I had no time to linger on any evaluation of Washington, DC, just now, as I aimed to hurry to my room and finish reading the clipping.

I reached my room, anxious to absorb this new find. I read the article, then reread it. A group of folks were under investigation for violent acts. They called themselves Vegetarians for Life. However, the article explained that they were tied to extreme measures to stop the trade in meat, especially beef. Apparently, they had agents around the country that aimed to sow fear within the cattle industry. They saw meat-eaters as evil doers who would bring an end to civilization. Some fellow named Elder Barnabas led them. His picture was included in the article. Elder Barnabas wore a hooded black cape that nearly covered his face. What could be seen appeared downright evil. Did folks actually follow this excuse for humanity? What sort of person would be so duped? The writer of the article called the organization a cult.

It was certifiably insane. To violently protest food, a

commodity that was the choice of each person who desired it, was downright crazy. Besides, most folks loved beef.

So, I found myself dealing with some anonymous vegetarian with an extreme agenda. I was piling up clues, but I needed to catch this man to end the bizarre behavior. Each steer killed was an expensive loss to ranchers. Scarier still, a rancher might eventually come upon this man, and it could end in gunplay. I carefully folded the clipping and stuffed it in my saddlebag.

Now, I had nothing against folks who didn't eat meat. That was their personal concern. But to wrap that in a cloak of deadly cult-like acts stood out beyond the pale. I didn't cotton to some crazed lunatic killing mine or anyone else's beeves. Aside from being our livelihood, I believed that meat in your diet was good for you. This cattle assassin must be brought to justice sooner rather than later. Besides, he was giving peace-loving vegetarians a bad name around these parts.

I changed clothes and headed to the Lone Star Saloon. Some grub, a drink, and casual conversation sounded right fine.

I stepped through the front batwing doors of the Lone Star Saloon. It was not unlike most western saloons. Sawdust coated its floor, the bar looked barely able to support an elbow leaning on it, and the place stunk of leather, sweat, and booze. The Lone Star hummed with conversations. A few men played card games. All drank.

My large form standing in the doorway drew no attention. I found it strange how they'd have noticed me instantly if I wore a badge. Badges seemed to serve as eye magnets. All the tables were occupied, so I strode over to the bar and ordered a beer.

"Can I get some grub here?" I asked the barkeep.

"Just chili, pard," he responded.

"That'll do." I sipped the beer and soon had a steaming bowl of chili in front of me.

I caught the bartender stealing glances at me as though trying to figure out whether he knew me.

Finally, he eased over. "You a lawman? Texas Ranger or somethin'?"

I wore no badge. Was it something about the way I carried myself? I swallowed a mouthful of chili. "Used to be."

"Pick'em every time," said the barkeep.

"Matter of fact, I'm a rancher and looking for someone," I ventured.

"Lots of folks travel through Victoria. I do see a few. Got a name?" he asked, friendly-like.

"No name. Fellow wears black, rides a pale horse, plays Solitaire, and doesn't eat beef," I offered by way of a summary description.

"Don't eat beef? Dang, I'd remember some idiot like that!" He thought a minute. "Can't say as I recall anyone lookin' like you describe." He refilled my beer. "What you lookin' for him for?"

"In addition to not eating beef, he's been killing cattle around South Texas. Got one of mine, and I'm determined to put him out of business," I responded.

"Shucks, I can think of plenty of folks who'd sign on to a posse," said the barkeep.

"Well, I'm not looking to hang him, but I do yearn to bring him in."

"Good luck, pard. If I hear or see anything, should I call you?" he asked.

"Thanks. Let Sheriff Heck know." I finished off the chili and took a generous gulp of beer. "What do I owe you?"

"On the house, pard. Chili is free to the law. Once a Ranger, always a Ranger. Good luck with your hunt." He smiled and went off to serve another customer.

I left a tip and headed out. There were three other saloons to check out.

The Fashion Saloon and the Gem Saloon didn't pan out, but life got interesting in the Ruby Saloon. It was getting late. The only men around were those still drinking. By now, most had drunk too much.

I was standing at the bar, sipping my fifth beer of the evening and feeling a slight buzz myself. I was determined to not finish this one. I'd learned nothing of my quarry from the bartender and was absentmindedly gazing around the room. As with the other drinking establishments, this one was full of smells of cigar and cigarette smoke, along with the combined aromas of sweat, leather, and booze.

One of the cowboys sitting at a table and playing too many losing poker hands didn't take kindly to my scanning the room. He stood, said something nasty to one of the men he was in the game with, and walked to the bar. He stood about four or five feet from me. "Barkeep! Gimme another brew!" he demanded loudly enough to momentarily silence the room.

I had my back to the bar and caught him in my peripheral vision.

"What the hell you lookin' at?" he groused. He was a fair-sized man, though I had perhaps four inches in height and thirty pounds on him. I guessed him at maybe twenty years old. He was wearing what he might have fancied was the *great equalizer* in a holster on his hip.

"You talking to me?" I asked politely. I gave him my best *don't mess with me* look.

The cowboy didn't read my eyes. He took a step toward me with one hand pulled back to throw a punch.

He never saw my fist coming. Next thing everyone in the saloon knew, a body lay flat out on the barroom floor.

"Damn!" hollered the bartender from behind me. "Nobody ever cold-cocked Slim Dixon before!"

I was glad the drunken cowboy hadn't gone for his gun. That would not likely have ended so well for him or me. I glanced around the room to be sure there was no further trouble, then turned to the barkeep and laid a couple of silver dollars on the bar. "When your friend comes to, feed him and tell him no hard feelings." With that, I left my unfinished beer and headed back to the hotel. I reckoned I'd had about enough of Victoria. Time to head home.

# NINE
# WRONG PLACE, WRONG TIME

MCTAVISH RODE easy-like through prairie flatlands lit only by a blanket of stars. He had figured that working in daylight was getting ever-riskier, as folks began guarding against him the best they could. Eventually, it meant encountering some ranch hand. He had his mission and had been keeping his cadre of co-conspirators informed of his efforts. He'd read a couple of local newspapers but seen nothing of his exploits. Surely, the ranchers must be having second thoughts about raising cattle. They must realize that with raising cattle and producing meat, they were delivering an evil that fed the fires of evil. People had to be dissuaded from eating meat, or it would spell the end of the civilized world. Of this, McTavish was convinced. Hadn't Elder Barnabas assured him of the sanctity of his mission in preventing the End Times, Armageddon, Apocalypse? The meat-eaters were going to lead mankind into the sins that would signal the end.

Once in Texas, he'd avoided lingering near any one place. By his count, he'd killed fourteen beeves thus far. He saw himself as far from finished. Texas was a long way from the heathers of Scotland and his adopted home near Washington, DC. He'd come to America to seize opportunity, but he'd failed here as he had in his homeland. He'd become a desperate reject of society; living in squalor and poor as a church mouse. He had no wife, no children, and, alas, no love.

He'd come to hate the world that he blamed for taking everything from him. He felt cheated again and again. He bore a major grudge. Then one day, as he sat on a park bench, a saintly-looking man in black robes approached him. So began his rising from the ashes of self-defeat. Elder Barnabas filled him with purpose. He cast aside eating meat at his priestly benefactor's urging. Elder Barnabas had found a willing disciple for Vegetarians for Life, instilling his own deep-rooted passions for the evils of eating red meat. It wasn't enough to simply not eat meat. Elder Barnabas believed that meat and the cattle that produced it spelled the end of the world. The Great Apocalypse; Armageddon would descend upon everyone.

McTavish and a handful of other disciples would be destined to go among the cattle ranches and save the world. Oh, it sounded insane to anyone with common sense, but the likes of Ambrose McTavish were sucked into its gaping maw. He'd been beaten into a deranged shadow that grasped passionately at the teachings of Elder Barnabas. McTavish had been given a purpose.

An evil grin rivaling the serpent in the Garden of Eden creased his chin as he wondered what ranchers might think of the apocalyptic design on the back of the playing cards. That had been his idea, and he hoped it delivered his message.

My trip to Beeville and Victoria had been reasonably successful. Clues were coming together. It was slow work, but I found myself encouraged. If this cattle assassin figured he could get away with his killings, he was dead wrong. The killer had sorely misjudged the heart and soul of Texans. Eventually, this killer would make a mistake. Lawbreakers invariably made a mistake that resulted in capture or death. However, I didn't figure on either of those outcomes just yet, unless my hand was forced.

I had to admit that it was going to take all of my cunning to root this man out. I was determined that justice would prevail. Aside from the money I was being paid, I reminded myself that I had a personal stake in this. The man had killed one of my beeves just for the sake of killing it. In Texas or most anywhere, that was a hanging offense.

Life occasionally offers coincidences, and this day managed to come up with one. I'd decided to ride on through my cousin Nick Dunn's ranch. Nick was getting on in years, but had built a reputation as a cattle speculator and had life experiences that some thought made him legendary. I guess homesteading at fifteen, driving cattle to market, being known as a superb Comanche fighter, and raising nine children was pretty doggone special.

I encountered a barbed wire fence, so followed it until I found a gate and could let myself through. I rode for a half mile or so until I reached the top of a hill. I looked up and saw buzzards circling. Naturally curious, I urged Tornado forward to see what they were interested in.

Before long, I found myself in a dry arroyo directly under those circling birds. Tornado's ears pricked up, and I smelled the aroma of death. I'd been upwind, but had now gotten close enough to pick up the smell. I also heard the growls and yips of some other scavengers that the buzzards were hoping would soon leave. I wasn't excited about dealing with hungry coyotes, but they were cowardly beasts for the most part.

A little farther, and I came upon a horrible scene. There was a dead steer and, sadly, more. A saddled horse was standing near the body of what looked to be a dead cowboy. He was likely one of Nick's hands. The cowboy had been nearly cut in two at the waist. What sort of weapon did that? Glancing at the steer, it bore the *modus operandi* of the cattle assassin. It appeared that the cowboy came upon the killer at work and suffered for his curiosity. I saw his gun belt lying nearby with the gun still in its holster. The cowboy apparently hadn't had a chance to use it.

I wrapped my bandana over my nose and dismounted to have a closer look. The man's horse didn't move. Examining him, I didn't figure to simply wrap him in a blanket and tie him over the saddle, because there were two pieces of him. I reckoned there wasn't an ounce of blood remaining in the cowboy's body. I had no choice. I fetched the man's bedroll, wrapped both halves of him in the blanket, and managed to tie the bundle on his horse's saddle.

Lawmen are occasionally called upon to kill a lawbreaker, usually in self-defense. Just as my dad, I'd had to answer that call more often than I'd cared to. I'd investigated murder scenes as well. Nothing I'd ever seen was as stomach-churningly heinous as what had been done to the cowboy.

I took a final scan of the area and found the telltale playing card. Seeing nothing more of note, I headed Tornado toward Nick's house with the cowboy's cayuse in tow. The stakes had suddenly changed. Now, I was pursuing a murderer.

☆☆

As I rode, I mulled over all the clues I'd gathered to date. I was frustrated, to put it mildly. The case had just taken on a new intensity. Killing cattle would send the perpetrator to jail. Murder rose to a higher level. The cattle killer would hang for his deed, though I thought it to be far too easy an end for him, given the horror of the manner in which he killed Nick's cowhand.

I didn't feature having to tell Cassie about this. There was no way to sugar-coat the deed, and it was only fair that she knew what her husband was dealing with.

Try as I might, I was unable to get inside the cattle killer's head. Grasping the crazed mindset, the sickness of the man, defied my senses. Try as I might, I couldn't put myself there. What power did the cult offer that motivated a man to such depths of depravity? What misplaced powers of persuasion did Elder Barnabas employ? Questions, questions, and more questions.

I racked my brain trying to figure a way to entrap this murderous cattle killer.

Sheriff McTiernan was none-too-pleased when he learned of the murder. His distress was about more than the grisly nature of the deed. Other crimes paled in comparison to the very personal crime of murder. Citizens might be numbed to the likes of disorderly conduct, petty theft, rustling, or even assault, but murder was another matter altogether. McTiernan would be pressured to bring the perpetrator to justice.

My cousin Nick had seen a lot during his fifty years in Texas. While he'd witnessed the results of horrible Comanche tortures and heard tales of cannibalistic tribes, the murder of his ranch hand was at another level. That he'd been killed by a man who appeared to be some sort of crazed cattle killer weighed especially heavy.

The toughest part turned out to be that the cowboy had a family. He lived with his wife and three kids near Corpus Christi and spent several days a week at Nick's ranch. I figured to leave it to my cousin to deal with the grief that was sure to come. It seemed better for the family to hear the news from Nick rather than a stranger.

However, Nick was a fiery sort and was of a mind to raise a posse. It took the best of my persuasive powers to calm his Irish temper enough to give up the idea. Vigilantism wasn't the answer. The murderer would be long gone by now, and we had no idea who he was or where he might have gone. I left Nick with my promise to see that justice was done. Justice invariably defied death.

# TEN
# THE BADGE CALLS

HOW MANY TIMES would Cassie tolerate my pinning that Texas Ranger badge back on my shirt? I promised that I'd hung it up for good the last time. I committed to her and Heaven's Gate Ranch, being husband, father, and provider. Dare I even ask? Yet, if I found the perpetrator and had to shoot him, it would create a decidedly dicey situation legally and morally. I'd have no authority to arrest the man.

The house—our home—looked right fine as I approached. I headed Tornado straight to the barn. He'd earned a good currying and oat feed. Hiding under the habit of any cowboy worth his salt caring for his horse above all else gave me time to more think on what I'd tell Cassie.

I finally finished with Tornado, patted him, and headed up to the bog house. I strode confidently up the steps to the gallery and pushed open the front door. I froze at the click of a shotgun hammer being cocked.

"Lucas! Thank God I look before I shoot," she said with relief. She lowered the shotgun and stepped into my arms.

After a few moments of welcoming hugs, she led me into the kitchen, where our children were busy playing.

I was soon sitting at the kitchen table savoring the coffee Cassie poured for me.

"So, was your journey productive?" she asked.

I nodded. "I learned a lot in Beeville. I'm getting a pretty-fair picture of who and what I'm dealing with. He apparently belongs to some cult-like organization of vegetarians back in Washington, DC. It seems pretty clear that the man isn't right in his head." I took a long sip of the hot coffee and dropped my head between my hands.

"Something else happened?" pressed Cassie.

"He killed a cowhand on Nick's ranch." I lamented.

Cassie's jaw dropped. "No!" She burst into tears.

"Yeah. Sam Eddings, one of Nick's top hands, apparently happened upon the cattle assassin as he was killing a steer." I wiped my eyes, which were feeling teary. "The man had a wife and children." A tear found its way down my cheek, then a couple more. I suppose it had taken until now for the murder to impact me.

By now, Sean and Bode realized that something serious was going on with their folks. They toddled over to do their level best to offer comfort. Naturally, baby Carolyn broke the spell with a hungry wail.

"Must you?" As Cassie comforted Carolyn, she was asking whether I was taking up the badge again.

I shook my head. "I don't think so. You've been good about it, sweetheart. I'm sticking to my promise. If I must, I'll pull in Sheriff McTiernan." Somehow, that didn't ring true. If confronted, I might very well be forced to deal with the cattle assassin myself. With the murder of Nick's cowhand, coupled with the killing of my own steer, this had become personal to me. Though I refused to renege on my promise to Cassie about pinning on the badge, this had gone beyond me going solo. It had become clear that additional resources were needed.

Cassie gazed at me through tear-reddened eyes and smiled. "What's next?"

"You're full of questions," I chided, then winced as I realized I was being a tad insensitive. "Good question," I said softly. I leaned back and took a sip of coffee while ruffling Sean's hair. "Where are Brody and Tess?" I strove to change the subject, as I really hadn't decided on what my next move would be.

Cassie gave me one of those stern looks that told me to answer the question. She wanted action.

"Expect I should let Archie Parr know what's going on," I responded.

"Telephone call?" She knew the answer before she asked the question.

"Too sensitive for that. I'd better go see him. I'll do it tomorrow morning." I emptied the coffee cup. "Meanwhile, I'd better go and let Jake, Jimmy, and Pedro in on what happened."

I looked as lovingly as I could muster into Cassie's eyes. "I'm still cogitating on what I specifically plan to do." I'd been honest, and she appreciated it. Her sitting there in all her sweet beauty, nursing Carolyn, reinforced my decision to let the law deal with bringing in the cattle assassin. I'd do what I could to earn what they were paying me, but I would avoid confronting the murderer.

I reckoned to go for a ride and was headed to the barn when Jimmy came galloping in hard. "Mr. Dunn!" he hollered upon seeing me.

I stopped mid-stride as he pulled up his lathered horse

in a cloud of dust. "Yuh gotta come to your mom's house. Come quick!"

"What's up?" I asked. His urgency had my full attention.

"She ain't well," he nearly hollered.

I ran to saddle Tornado. I wished Jimmy had used the telephone, but he couldn't bring himself to accept the device. There was too much cowboy in him. "Go tell Cassie to bring the kids to Mom's house. Be calm, Jimmy. Don't be stirring her up." Mom had been under the weather, but she was a strong woman, so I wasn't concerned. "Tell her to call the doc," I called out, as I cinched Tornado's saddle.

I was soon a bolt of lightning dashing up the lane toward my mom's house. I fairly leaped from the saddle, hitched Tornado, and brought myself up short. I needed to collect myself. Dusting myself off, I climbed the steps and entered my mom's home. "Mom?" I called out. I knew very well where she was. If she was ailing, she never took to her bed. She'd be in the parlor, sitting in a big rocker.

I headed up the hallway and strode into the parlor. I could see her sitting in that rocker on the far side of the room, looking out the window at the vast reaches of the ranch.

"Junior, darling? That you?" came a weak voice.

I eased on over beside her. She looked deathly pale; not a good sign at all. Each breath seemed to be a struggle and was accompanied by a wheezing sound. "Mother?" How are you?" It was a perfunctory question, and I knew it. I leaned in and hugged her.

Weak as her hug was, she didn't release me. She finally let me pull back and looked up at me through red-rimmed eyes. "I love you, Lucas," she said. She'd always called me Junior. This was the first time she'd called me by my dad's name.

"I love you, too, Mom," I replied with my hand lying gently on her arm.

With a trembling hand, she grasped an envelope from the table beside her. "This is for you, Lucas." She handed it to me. "You can open it."

I paused, wondering what this was about, before opening the envelope. I read the codicil to the Last Will and Testament of Elisa Corrigan Dunn. A deed was attached. I nearly dropped it as I read the first paragraph. Edward Thorpe, a wealthy financier whom my dad had helped and who had given his own ranch holdings to my mom and dad to oversee, had deeded the entire property to me upon my mom's passing. My jaw dropped. "What about my brothers and sisters?"

Mom was fading. "They're provided for, Lucas."

I heard Cassie enter the house with our children.

"Back here, sweetheart," I called out.

She swept into the room with baby Carolyn in her arms just as my mom's hands went limp.

Mom looked up at Cassie. "You got a good one, daughter." They were her final words.

Cassie and I sat on a settee near my mom for a while. Sean and Bode sensed that it was a quiet moment. There was no fussing from them. A couple of hours later, the doctor arrived and formally pronounced my mom as having died. It had the heavy feel of finality to it.

"Shall I take her back to Nuecestown, Junior?" asked the doc.

"We'll bury her right here at Heaven's Gate beside my dad," I replied. Thanks for coming.

With the doc gone, we were alone with the children again. I realized that I'd have to reach out to my brothers and sisters.

"What's that on the table, Lucas?" asked Cassie.

I'd placed the codicil on the table when I realized that Mom was struggling to breathe. I handed it to Cassie.

"Oh, my!" she gasped.

"Three hundred and fifty thousand acres." I summed it up for her. The deeded property had significantly expanded our holdings. It added a couple of more ranch hands to the payroll in addition to several hundred head of cattle.

There was a knock at the door.

"Come in," I invited.

Jimmy, Pedro, and Jake walked in, followed by Carlos and Rance, my mom's ranch hands.

"Glad you fellows are here. We'll need to dig a grave." I hated that word. "It should be beside my dad. If y'all will be kind enough to harness the wagon, I'll carry her to it."

The hands scrambled to get the wagon.

We were soon gathered about the grave. The plot had grown over the years from first being the final resting place of my mom's mother, father, and brother, to my dad, a couple of miscarriages, and a brother and sister. It was a lovely spot overlooking the prime pasture lands of Heaven's Gate Ranch.

I led a funeral service as best I could. While we'd studied the Good Book as I'd grown up and my dad had actually courted my mom at a church picnic, we weren't church-going folks. The closest church was better than a half-day ride away. So, I did the best I could. There were plenty of tears as Elisa Corrigan Dunn sank into Texas soil.

When the last spade full of soil was placed on my mom's grave, I sprinkled rose petals over it. The rose petals had been an annual ritual of hers to recognize the death of her parents at the hands of a Comanche raiding party.

As Cassie and I walked hand-in-hand from the little family plot, I felt as though I had suddenly become a new man. With my parents gone and my remaining brothers and sisters far from here, I became the preserver of the Dunn legacy. Despite being the youngest, I had become the elder statesman of the family ranching legacy.

With the funeral behind us and all the myriad estate tasks associated with the passing of my mom, I could finally get back to focusing on the case. After much consideration, I appointed Jake as ranch foreman. This served to ease the operational burdens from my shoulders.

We thought about whether it made sense to move to the house my mom and dad had built, but we were comfortable where we were. We salvaged some furniture and memorabilia, then ultimately decided to turn the place into a guest house for family visits. A couple of my older married sisters did visit, and we let them take a few items that held meaning for them. In no time, everything was settled.

I had leveled with our ranch hands about the murder on Nick's ranch and the risks now entailed in sticking around Heaven's Gate Ranch. They reckoned that they'd endured Comanche and Apache raids, dealt with Mexican bandits, and harsh weather, so they viewed the cattle assassin as just another hazard of the job.

I was soon headed to San Diego to personally bring Archer Parr up to date. Tornado was well rested from our journey to Beeville and Victoria, so I picked up our pace to an energetic walk. I rather looked forward to Parr's reaction. Would he pull back on my assignment or push for more? I expected the latter. That was the sort of man he was —or had become.

My thinking turned to next steps. How was I to pin down this murderer? I'd tracked men and beasts, but this prey was more like some mirage. Folks came upon his kills by pure chance. Even if he left signs on a trail, they might be days old and lead nowhere. I considered reaching out to ranches that hadn't been victimized yet. We might set traps, but that seemed chancy at best. How many would have to be set, and what were the chances of success? Such an effort would tie up ranch hands on what were likely time-consuming fools' errands. Yet, there must be some way to draw this psychopath in.

It occurred to me that he must be telling someone of his escapades. Was he communicating with this Elder Barnabas mentioned in the newspaper clipping? If so, how? If by telephone, he'd have to find a place that had one. Telegraph was a possibility, but from where? The mail was also possible, but the same dilemma existed. I wondered whether anyone back in Washington was tracking correspondence to Elder Barnabas? Did they even know or care? As I thought on it, this seemed to be a job for Parr to inquire about.

I finally reined in at Parr's office. I was ever underwhelmed at its modesty, though it was well-appointed inside.

Parr greeted me with his usual charm. "Welcome, Junior. Sorry about your mother." He paused graciously before getting to the business at hand. "Been looking forward to getting an update."

We shook hands, and I poured myself some coffee before grabbing a seat. This time, we sat at a round mahogany table opposite his desk. "Well, I do have encouraging news, Archer. Some not so much."

Parr lit a cigar. "Oh?"

I took my time and took a purposely slow sip of coffee. Parr was dripping with anticipation. "The cattle assassin is connected with an outfit called Vegetarians for Life headquartered in Washington, DC. It's apparently run by some fellow named Elder Barnabas. They are dedicated to turning the folks into vegetarians."

Parr nearly coughed as he took a pull on the cigar. "Vegetarians for Life?" he exclaimed. "Weird, Junior. That's plain weird."

"Not so weird. I believe it's like a cult, and this cattle assassin is a disciple. For all I know, there may be others. Texas isn't the only place raising beeves." I paused and enjoyed another sip of coffee while Parr gathered his wits and blew a perfect smoke ring skyward. "So, a barkeep in Beeville did see the man, but couldn't recall much, so far as physical description, other than slender but with broad shoulders and an unfriendly disposition. The man played Solitaire and refused to eat beef. He wore black and rode a pale gray horse. The barkeep said that some sort of device hung from the horse's saddle. From his description, I suspect it's a scythe. I doubt he's figuring to cut grass."

"Well, you've gathered quite a bit, Junior. What's next?" pressed Parr.

"There's more, Archer." Now, I grew especially serious. "I was cutting through my cousin Nick's property and happened upon a grisly scene. One of his cowhands happened upon the killer at a fresh steer kill and paid for it with his life. The sonofabitch sliced the cowboy in two at the waist."

Parr's jaw dropped. He nearly choked on his cigar again.

"I took the body to Nick, then contacted Sheriff McTiernan," I added.

"What now?" asked Parr.

"Washington," I stated flatly. "Is anyone in Washington watching this outfit? If not, they sure as shootin' ought to be."

"What do you expect me to do?" queried Parr.

He couldn't be serious! Here was a man with political aspirations, and he's clueless as to the politics of this. "Er, I rather thought this would be your territory. I mean, I'd charge Hell with a bucket of cold water but not Congress." Was I really having to explain his role?

Parr cleared his throat. He watched one of his smoke circles float toward the ceiling and disappear, then another. Finally, he took a final pull and extinguished the cigar. "You go back out there and track this lunatic. I'll sort out the Washington end. It's a tad sticky, as Representative Rudolph Kleberg is Robert's brother. With Bob looking to keep a low profile in this, I'll have to check with him first. If need be, I could give one of our senators, Culberson or Chilton, a holler. I'll handle the political end. They may know whether other ranchers are facing the same sort of problem we are."

That was closer to the sort of answer I was seeking. "Sounds good. I suppose you realize that I'm walking a fine line here," I advised.

Parr stood. "If we didn't think you could handle it, we wouldn't have hired you. That about right, Junior?" He extended his hand. "I suppose you'd like to see whether our beloved elected representatives can come up with a name. I'll try."

"Of course. Good to see you, Archie." I shook Parr's hand and exited. I had my marching orders, so to speak. While I awaited any news from Parr's inquiry to Robert Kleberg's brother, I had to figure a way to find this cattle assassin.

I did feel the pull of that Texas Ranger badge calling me from the dresser drawer. So far, my oath was winning the tug-of-war. There was no point in hanging around San Diego, so I lit out for home. There was a full moon, so a night ride over familiar territory wouldn't be so bad.

McTavish found himself facing an unexpected turn of events. That cowboy showing up had changed everything. Of course, he had to be killed. McTavish couldn't afford witnesses. Sanely applied logic told him to put distance between himself and South Texas. However, he was a man caught up in the passion of an agenda that he saw as far greater than his mortal being. Emotion trumped rationality.

He decided to lie low for a few days. He had plenty of supplies, and there were places not so far off where cattle had yet to experience his deadly scythe. There were plenty of ranches and even towns that hadn't felt his might. He couldn't kill all the cattle, but he'd kill enough to give those ranchers second thoughts about raising the denizens of mankind's downfall.

The consequence of McTavish's habit of isolation was that he was unaware of who, if anyone, was pursuing him. Surely, the murder of the cowboy would put the law on his trail. The scythe had been his weapon of choice. It had been ideal as a symbol of his duty. As the scythe cut the grass, so it would shear the cattle industry at its very roots. Now? Perhaps it made sense to obtain a gun. Yes, he'd have to see to that.

# ELEVEN
# UNEXPECTED THREAT

I AWOKE EARLY next morning with Cassie snuggled tightly beside me. I'd snuck in well after midnight and shed my spurs and boots. I strove to be especially quiet so as not to disturb anyone and was glad that I'd tightened up those creaky stairs. I gazed lovingly at her. She'd likely gone to bed not expecting me until next day. I'd give odds that she hadn't even awakened when I slipped under the blankets.

I gave Cassie a kiss atop her head and crawled out of bed. I put on enough clothes to be presentable and headed downstairs to brew some coffee. Soon, I was sitting on the gallery out front with my feet propped up on the railing and a hot brew in my hands. My spurs fit neatly into the notches my dad's spurs had worn into the gallery railing over many years. It was thinking time.

Progress on this case had been decidedly slow, as so many unknowns were hanging in the fog that at times accompanies a manhunt. I once again tried to put myself in the murderer's head, but how do you get yourself inside the thoughts of a nutcase? The man seemed unpredictable. The closest thing to a pattern was the opportunity to kill a steer, and that was random. I was still haunted by when and how he was reaching Elder Barnabas. Whoever the cattle assassin was, he was out there roaming around close to seven thousand square miles of Texas landscape. There was no shortage of places for him to hide.

I wondered at the tool the cattle assassin was using. It surely wasn't the sort of scythe someone would use to trim grass or brush. It had to be razor sharp with the heft to drive deep into a steer—or cut a man in two. I shuddered at the thought of what had happened to Nick's cowhand. He'd been at the right place at the wrong time.

I had begun to think that while setting a trap might be a possible way to capture the man, I might have better luck getting the word out to the saloons. If the murderer in fact played Solitaire, an optimal place to play would be a table at a saloon. I decided to chat with McTiernan about getting wanted posters out to the owners of the saloons in the area. He could pass them along to other lawmen for them to distribute. The only downside was that I didn't want to flush the man out of South Texas. It wouldn't do to foist him on ranches farther away and make my job of pursuit more difficult owing to less familiar territory. Aside from personal commitment, I still had the balance of the ten thousand dollars to earn.

"You hungry, cowboy?" called Cassie from the front door. She'd whipped up breakfast while I was cogitating.

I had no sooner sat at the kitchen table with a second cup of coffee, when the telephone rang. "I'll get it," I called to Cassie as she dished up flapjacks and venison sausage. I fumbled a moment with the danged device, as I really wasn't used to it. "Hello? Luke Dunn here."

"Luke? It's Archer," came a voice that sounded far off. "Ambrose McTavish is the man's name."

"McTavish?" I repeated.

"Rudy Kleberg says there are a couple of psychos like McTavish killing beeves in Colorado. They're using poison. The Feds are keeping an eye on Elder Barnabas. Looks like they're going to arrest him but need enough evidence to build a case. Kleberg appreciated knowing about the murder. That took investigations up a notch. That's about it. Go get him, Junior." There was a click. Telephone calls didn't usually last too long. Aside from other folks wanting to use lines, there were always eavesdroppers.

"Who was it?" asked Cassie, as I returned to the table and her delicious flapjacks drowned in maple syrup from back east.

"Archer Parr gave me the name of the murderer. Seems there are some others like him in Colorado." I stuffed a piece of flapjack dripping with syrup into my mouth. "Oh, the murderer is a fellow named Ambrose McTavish."

"So, you have a name, a description, and what I've heard you call a *modus operandi*. What's next?" Cassie had narrowed the situation down to basics.

"I was thinking about a wanted poster and reward."

"That'll chase him away, Lucas," she said with an assurance that startled me. "And given what happened to that cowboy, anyone approaching him could be at risk." She was right, of course.

"I thought about setting a trap, but that has a snowball's chance in hell of working." I paused to take a sip of coffee. "I suppose getting the word out to saloons and restaurants with a warning to avoid confronting McTavish makes the best sense."

Cassie smiled and nodded. "At least if a barkeep calls, you can follow up. Maybe, there'll be a trail to follow."

She could make a whole lot of sense, and I fully appreciated Cassie narrowing my approach. Finding McTavish was like the proverbial needle in a haystack. As to getting the word out to saloons, by the time I was notified, McTavish would likely be long gone. Still, it was worth trying. "Thanks, sweetheart," I said with gratitude in my tone. Just then, Sean grabbed my leg. "Horsey, Daddy?" This was the world I loved. Getting rid of McTavish would sure make it easier to fully appreciate.

I had copies made of a flyer I created with McTavish's description, including a warning that he was dangerous. I also included my telephone number. Jimmy, Jake, and Pedro agreed to distribute the flyers to saloons for a few extra dollars. I was right proud of myself for coming up with the scheme, albeit with Cassie's urging.

Meanwhile, I spent the next couple of weeks roaming around the ranch, finding stray longhorns and doing the sorts of chores typical to ranching life. Cassie kept me well fed, the kids were a joy, and our life in the bedroom was especially passionate. We even managed a liaison or two at the old swimming hole. With children and ranch hands around, those little getaways were a bit more challenging than when it was just the two of us on the ranch. I recalled my dad slyly telling me that he romanced my mother at the swimming hole. Naturally, I couldn't visualize that. Anyway, I suppose the swimming hole was sort of a family legacy.

With the flyers in the process of being distributed and ranch life at hand, I decided one day to ride to the far southern boundary of the ranch. It was September, so it was slightly cooler, mostly thanks to breezes crossing the prairies from the gulf. I'd begun to figure that McTavish was lying low for a bit, following the murder. I couldn't just lie around waiting for some bartender to call.

Tornado and I were fully enjoying the fresh air. I saw a few longhorns grazing, but there seemed no reason to disturb them. It was getting toward midday when I reckoned it was time to head home. I'd just turned Tornado northward when a loud bawling came from an arroyo perhaps a hundred yards off. I heard a growl and scuffling from behind some scrub bushes. The scuffling grew along with ever-louder bawling. I put spurs to Tornado and headed off to save what I figured to be a longhorn in distress.

I plunged through the brush and came upon a black bear attacking a calf. The cow was beside herself trying to protect the young critter. She bawled and tried to use her horns against the bear. Every time a horn got close, the bear swiped it away. The cow got lucky once with a horn, but it wasn't nearly enough to stop the bear. The calf was struggling and looked to be in rough shape already. The black bear? He was good-sized and nasty. I drew my Smith & Wesson and fired two shots into the air. The bear stopped, gave me a look, and then plunged back into his effort to kill himself a meal.

Tornado was holding steady, but just jittery enough that it would be hard to get a good shot off with my Winchester without hitting the calf or the cow. I dismounted and drew my rifle from its scabbard. I truly hated having to kill the bear, but once it tasted beef—if it hadn't already—it would be part of his diet going forward. I had to move quickly. Finding a position that offered a clear field of view, I chambered a round, aimed at the bear, and squeezed off a round. The slug caught the bear in its shoulder. Now, he was angry. He released the calf and turned to me. He raised himself to his full height. He was just a little taller than me.

I tried to work the rifle lever, but it jammed open. I hit it with the palm of my hand. It released but sent a bullet skyward. This gave the bear time to decide that I might make a better dinner. He hadn't taken kindly to that slug in his shoulder. Lowering himself to all fours, the big boar began his charge at me. Now, a black bear can reach a speed of around thirty miles per hour. With a mere forty or so feet between him and me, he began to close the gap quickly. He was too close for the Winchester, so I drew my Smith & Wesson and began pulling the trigger as fast as my finger permitted. I must have hit him at least a couple of times. I'd forgotten the two shots I'd fired into the air, and my hammer was soon striking empty casings.

The bear stopped. My bullets had stunned him. They might have been mortal wounds, but the bear didn't know that just yet. He sat a mere five or six feet from me with a decidedly angry look in his eyes. Enraged, he took a swipe at me but missed. He could do damage with those claws, though I was glad he wasn't a grizzly with its three-inch claws. I still had my Winchester in hand. I grabbed the barrel with both hands and gave the bear a tremendous whack on his snout and followed through with a second between his eyes. He stumbled and laid confused eyes on me. The dumb beast was stunned, hurt, and hadn't a clue as to why. I actually felt sorry for the dazed beast. As we stared eyeball to eyeball, the effects of my bullets began to kick in. The poor fellow finally gave me a bewildered look, breathed his last, and sank lifelessly in front of me.

I shook off my momentary trance and strode over to the calf. Its momma was licking the poor thing as it stood trembling and bleeding. Its little bleats were a sad commentary on what had just happened. I examined the little fellow. Would I have to mercy kill him, or would he survive? The bleeding was easing. It appeared he'd actually pull through this trauma without me lugging him back home with me. I decided to let momma longhorn handle it.

I'd been taught to always reload my weapons as soon as possible after any engagement. In this case, my black bear might have had a mate nearby. I reloaded and scanned the area. There didn't appear to be any other bears, so I put my revolver and carbine away.

Meanwhile, there was the matter of the dead black bear. I decided he should have a useful end. I reckoned he'd make a fine rug before our fireplace, generously donate his fat for lubricant, and actually make for some good eating, so I field dressed him and tied him behind Tornado. Much as we've been together for many years, my big stallion was none too pleased. Of course, he got over it.

Double-checking the injured calf, I figured he looked as though he'd pull through just fine. I was pleased to be heading for home. It was about this time that my senses were momentarily caught in how close I'd come to wrestling a six-hundred-pound apex hunter. An involuntary shudder swept through me. The outcome might not have been very pleasant had I not been able to shoot him.

McTavish figured that he's waited enough. It was time to get back to business. He hadn't heard from Elder Barnabas, but neither had he housed himself at a place with a telephone. An abandoned shack had been home for the past ten days. He had plenty of food and enjoyed hours of Solitaire.

He'd found a creek where he was able to wash that fool cowboy's blood from his clothes. The dried blood was difficult to see against the blackness of his cape, but he knew it was there. It was not only human blood but also from a mammal. He scrubbed away every stain.

He'd heard nothing of the impact his killings were having. That, combined with no communication with Elder

Barnabas, meant that he needed to find a newspaper and a telephone.

Jake was first to see me coming up the lane toward the big house. "Dang, boss! Where'd you get him?" he exclaimed.

I smiled. I suppose I could deliver an insufferably satisfied smile now and again. This one drooled conquest. "He had a hankering for one of our calves. We fought; I won."

Jake laughed and was soon joined by Jimmy and Pedro.

"You gonna make a rug?" asked Jimmy.

I nodded. "Pedro, would you kindly take this beast while I see to Tornado. Y'all can share the meat and bear fat with me." I paused. "Did y'all get those flyers distributed?"

"Yep. No problem, boss," replied Jimmy. "We told the barkeepers to not try to waylay the killer but to call you."

"Thanks." I hoped there were no ambitious bartenders who would risk their lives against McTavish. With the bear offloaded, I led Tornado into the stable and settled him. Once I tended to him, I walked nonchalantly to our house and entered quietly.

"Welcome home, Lucas. What was the ruckus about?"

"Nothing much," I said, doing a poor job of hiding my little ruse.

"What happened? Not McTavish?" she asked.

"Worse," I said teasingly.

She stood with her hands on her hips with anticipation.

"A black bear was after one of our calves. I had to kill the bear." I said evenly.

"Is the calf all right?"

"Yep. Momma longhorn is happy with her little one. The bear? Pedro is taking care to divide up the spoils. Bear steaks would make for a pleasant change of diet." I laughed. "Oh, and I reckoned a bearskin rug in front of the fireplace might be nice."

"Ummm, nice indeed," responded Cassie with a provocative tone.

I looked down at Sean and Bode. "I sure could use a couple of hugs and a cup of coffee in that order." With that, I swept the two boys off the ground and took a couple of spins with one in each arm.

# TWELVE
# PATIENCE CAN BE HELL

I HATE WAITING GAMES. I've always been an impatient sort, except when on an actual hunt for game. I suppose it's why I never took to fishing. The urge within me would be to grab a fish and make it bite the hook. With deer hunting, you often had to lie still to get a clear shot. I could manage that. This Ambrose McTavish waiting game was a grand test of my patience. Cassie felt the tension in me. Sean and Bode found me a bit less playful. Our ranch hands pretty much stayed clear of me. No question about it, patience can be hell—for everyone.

September gave way to October, and there were no sightings of McTavish. My cattle assassin did strike once at a ranch west of San Diego. Parr likely heard about it first but said nothing to me. The killing of another steer frustrated the hell out of me. I thought on the old joke about the buzzards circling around looking for carrion. Finally, one says to the other, "Patience, hell! I'm going to kill something!" I wished it were so easy.

There was a very much appreciated upside to hanging around Heaven's Gate Ranch. That old black bear made for a right nice little rug in front of our hearth. Cassie and I christened it and rechristened it a couple more times. There's something decidedly sexy about a naked woman wrapped in bearskin. No question that Cassie appreciated the naked me on that invitingly plush bearskin, and she showed it.

With the cooler weather, I reckoned that McTavish might ease back on his sick mission. Guess again, Lucas Dunn. In the space of the first two weeks of October, three more beeves were killed. McTavish's scythe was cutting a right-nasty swath through Texas cattle country.

I was getting less patient and more frustrated and angrier by the moment. I snapped at Pedro a couple of times over minor incidents. Jimmy and Jake made sure they were up and patrolling our pastures before I appeared on the gallery with my morning coffee. Cassie? She had to be the most tolerant wife on the face of the earth.

Just to fully test me, one morning I was sitting in my usual roost on the gallery sipping my pre-breakfast coffee, when I took a long gander out into the low-lying mist of distant pastures. McTavish! I'm sure it was the sonofabitch. He was riding across my ranch. The sheer audacity! Was I the only one to see him?

I nearly choked on my coffee. He'd be long gone by the time I saddled Tornado and gave chase. Where the hell was my old Sharps when I needed it? I'd have shown McTavish not to meddle with Texas beeves. And where were Jake and Jimmy? Damn!

I took a deep breath. I couldn't just sit here and watch him ride off. I tossed the rest of my coffee and poked my head in the door. "Keep breakfast warm, sweetheart. I have something to tend to." I ran to the stable. Poor Tornado was saddled about as fast as he'd ever been.

I was soon headed at a full gallop toward where I'd seen McTavish. I reined in at what I reckoned to be the spot. Nothing. No tracks. Not the least evidence of his presence. I circled around looking for sign, looking for anything that gave a hint at his having been here. I gazed around. I pulled my field glasses from my saddlebag and swept the horizon with them. Not a sign of McTavish. Had it been a mirage?

I sighed deeply. Was my patience running so thin that I was seeing things? Like that fish I wanted to force to bite the hook, I wanted to force McTavish into my hands. "Let's go, Tornado," I said resignedly, and we headed back home.

I gave Tornado some extra love. I'd put him through what turned out to be a wild goose chase, and he'd dutifully obliged. Currying Tornado gave me some thinking time while my hands were busy. I was just about finished, when an idea struck me. I decided to play a head game with Ambrose McTavish.

I headed to breakfast with a spring to my step and a devilish smile curling my lips.

"What's gotten into you?" asked Cassie.

"I came up with an idea to lure McTavish to me."

"And what do you have in mind, Lucas?" she asked.

I calmly took a bite from the warmed-up eggs and bacon. A biscuit slathered in butter and washed down with fresh coffee helped that. I exuded confidence. "I'm going to send notes to McTavish."

"Notes?"

"I reckon to post notes around the area with messages aimed at provoking McTavish to do something stupid, to make a critical mistake." I sipped my coffee. "You can help write them."

That brought a smile that turned to uncertainty. "You don't figure to invite him here, do you?" she asked.

I wanted no part of having that scythe anywhere near my family. "Simple. I'll tell him that I'll be waiting in Nuecestown."

"Well, when shall we begin writing?" Cassie was clearly enthused by the prospect of luring McTavish in and ending the stalemate.

"Grab some paper. Soon as I'm done eating, we'll get started." This was going to be fun. My mind began to churn with teases that might cause McTavish to look for me.

☆☆

As Cassie and I began to write, there was a knock at the door.

"I'll get it." I dropped my pen and headed for the door. I opened it to find an angry Jake staring back at me.

"The sonofabitch got another of our beeves, boss," he lamented.

I could see that Jake was seething with deeply held anger. "Sorry, Jake. But come on in. Cassie and I are working on something to capture McTavish."

He swiped off the trail dust with his hat and stepped inside. "What's up, boss?" He looked a tad perplexed that I wasn't more concerned about losing another longhorn, but he followed.

"We're setting traps," I said with a mischievous smile. I led Jake into the kitchen, where Cassie had already completed several messages. "Sit down and put your mind to luring McTavish in, Jake. We're hoping to get him to come to us."

I began reading the messages Cassie was creating. They were damned good. A couple especially caught my eye.

One read, "We know who you are. We love beef. See you in Nuecestown." Another read, "Texans love steak. Yummy. Lots of beef in Nuecestown." Still another read, "Elder Barnabas ate a steak. See you in Nuecestown." They were more than provocative. They were downright brilliant. The question remained as to whether they'd be enough to trap Ambrose McTavish.

My patience might have been wearing thin, but this ploy opened hope for ending the wait.

Jake, Jimmy, Pedro, and I now set about tying dozens of messages to shrubs in pastures around the region. It took a couple of days, but we figured that McTavish would eventually see at least one. Would it be enough to lure him in?

## THIRTEEN
# CLOSE, BUT...

I FIGURED to spend more time hanging out in Nuecestown. With any luck, this exercise wouldn't take but a handful of days to come to fruition. I felt cautiously optimistic.

I was getting Tornado saddled to ride to Nuecestown when Cassie called me to come to the telephone. I hustled to the house.

"It's somebody in Agua Dulce," she informed me.

I grabbed the mouthpiece. "Hello. This is Luke Dunn."

A voice came in hushed tones. "Mistuh Dunn. I be heah in Agua Dulce. A man like in yer postuh be settin' right heah in my saloon."

There was only one watering hole in tiny Agua Dulce. "I'll be there fast as I can. Please try to keep him there." The man hung up. I turned to Cassie. "He's there. I must ride!"

I ran back out to the stable and finished saddling Tornado. He caught my urgency and pranced excitedly in anticipation. I double-checked the loads in my Winchester carbine and Smith & Wesson revolver, mounted up, and headed west toward Agua Dulce.

☆☆

"Kin I git yuh some grub?" the barkeep asked.

McTavish had been drinking tea for the past couple of hours while he played Solitaire with his incessant snapping of the cards. He gave the barkeep a jaundiced eye. His morning had been spent looking for a likely target for his scythe, but he'd come up empty. There'd simply been too much risk, as he'd slept late and gotten a delayed start to his day. He was hungry, but also troubled. "What are you serving?" he asked.

"Git some fine beef tacos," suggested the barkeep. "The chili be good, too."

"You have any entrees without meat?" queried McTavish.

The barkeep gave him a look as though he must be crazy. "I expect I kin whip up a couple of taters."

"Do you have corn or some greens?" pursued McTavish.

The barkeep scratched his head. "If that'll keep yuh happy," he responded.

"Fine. I'll have some potatoes and whatever other vegetables you have." McTavish barely looked up from his cards.

"Them's fancy cards yuh got," observed the barkeep.

"I'm hungry," snarled McTavish with a steely gaze.

Knowing he must keep the man in his saloon, the barkeep chose not to further offend McTavish. He shook his head as he headed off to cook up the meatless fare.

McTavish sipped his tea and wrapped up another game of Solitaire. He dug into his pocket and pulled out a slip of paper. He read the challenge once again. "Come see me in Nuecestown. I've got a message from Elder Barnabas." What common sense he possessed told him it might be a trap and to stay clear of Nuecestown. This wasn't the way

Elder Barnabas reached out to him. In fact, his exalted leader never reached out. McTavish always initiated the communication. In fact, he'd tried to call Elder Barnabas twice this morning, and there was no answer.

McTavish looked at the doorway to the kitchen. The meal preparation was taking far too long. Something wasn't right.

Agua Dulce wasn't much so far as activity this day. The streets were empty, as local ranchers and farmers were preparing for the coming winter. McTavish was all-too-aware that winter spelled fewer targets as prime beeves had gone to market and those left behind were being bred and fattened up. One man had visited the saloon, bought a drink, gave him an appraising look, and departed with nary a word.

His meal still had not arrived.

McTavish put away his cards and headed out of the saloon. The streets were deadly quiet. It was as though folks had been warned to stay away. Even his eastern-ness told him to get out of town. He might be naïve as to the ways of the west, but he was no one's dummy. He'd been out here doing his foul deeds long enough to have developed some awareness of how these backward folks thought.

"Hey, where yuh goin'?" came a voice from behind him. "Yuh can't be leavin'."

McTavish gave the barkeep an angry look. "Eat it yourself," he snarled and mounted up. He put spurs to the gray horse and galloped northward from Agua Dulce.

★★

The ride from Heaven's Gate to Agua Dulce took better than four hours at a steady canter. I dared not push Tornado any harder.

I recognized that the chances of the barkeep detaining McTavish long enough for me to get there were slim to none. I relied on the slim chance.

It was mid-afternoon, when I pulled up to the only saloon in Agua Dulce. I hitched a heavy-breathing Tornado out front and headed for the entrance. It was a small establishment that looked to be nearly falling apart. It looked to be too cramped for my rifle to be effective, so I strode on in through the weather-beaten door with my hand on the butt of my Smith & Wesson revolver.

I stood aside so as to not be silhouetted in the doorway and blinked my eyes for a moment to adjust to the dimness inside. Two Mexican laborers sat at a table. Otherwise, the place was empty save for the barkeep, who stood behind the bar with a shrug and his arms spread wide in a pose of hopelessness.

"Did you call me about the wanted man?" I asked.

The barkeep nodded. "I tried tuh keep him, suh," he lamented. "Lit out an hour ago."

I shook my head, knowing that it had been a hopeless situation from the moment I'd left the ranch. "Thanks for trying. Which way did he head?"

"He be headin' north. He be a mean-lookin' sonofabitch," observed the barkeep.

I flipped him a dollar and headed back outside. I took a long look at Tornado. It'd be asking a lot to push him hard now. As to picking up McTavish's trail, a rainstorm was about to sweep in. Any tracks would be washed away. With a long sigh, I resigned myself to heading home.

As I mounted up, the barkeep appeared in the doorway. "Say," he called out. "Thet fella dropped this." He walked over and handed me a folded piece of paper. It was one of the messages we'd set out for McTavish.

So, he'd found one. It had grabbed him enough to

pocket it. Would he bite on the bait? Was he curious enough to throw caution to the wind and show up in Nuecestown? Well, I figured to head to Nuecestown and sit a spell. Just maybe he'd show up.

# FOURTEEN
# PURSUIT

I TOOK the time to call Sheriff McTiernan from Agua Dulce to let him know that I was headed to Nuecestown and springing a trap on the cattle assassin. He wasn't at his office, so I left a message with a deputy.

I didn't reckon the sheriff would be present when I finally met McTavish face-to-face in Nuecestown. With a message sent, I mounted Tornado and headed as fast as my beloved steed could carry me to Nuecestown.

Upon arrival, I headed to the Stagecoach Inn, where I unsaddled Tornado and gave him free-rein in the corral beside the building. I was breathing nearly as heavily as Tornado.

Well, lo and behold, I'll bet I hadn't parked my backside on the bench in front of the inn but thirty minutes, and a black-clothed rider on a pale horse came trotting up the main street. It was a tad muddy owing to that rainstorm that had come through, but it had to be McTavish looking to be none the worse for wear. He was an evil-looking sort of character with slits for eyes. I half expected to see a split tongue flick out from his mouth like a serpent. It appeared that Cassie had been right in her assessment. This man featured himself as one of the horsemen of the apocalypse. I recall her saying that death rode a pale horse.

He was bold. I'd give him that. He rode right on up to the inn, climbed from his saddle, and walked on past me into the inn. Being that it was mid-afternoon, only a couple of customers sat inside savoring whatever fine liquors they enjoyed this time of day.

I shrugged and double-checked the load in my Smith & Wesson. I reckoned to give McTavish a chance to get settled. If he had some expectation of a message from his Elder Barnabas, he'd surely prepare himself for a wait.

I'd already spoken to the bartender. He was to inform McTavish that he'd received a message from a man who called himself Elder Barnabas and to expect a disciple of some organization called Vegetarians for Life. Whether McTavish would grow suspect of the timing of such a message to coordinate with his arrival in Nuecestown remained to be seen.

Turning my head, I could see through the front window into the saloon section of the inn. I watched, as McTavish walked up to the bar and spoke with the barkeep. I was unable to hear, but the barkeep apparently delivered my message. Then, dang his soul, he stole a side glance at me. McTavish caught the glance and saw me watching. It didn't take him but a moment to figure that it was a trap. Any idiot could have put that together. McTavish might have been on a fool's errand and mentally a tad out of plumb, but he wasn't totally stupid.

McTavish looked for an escape. His eyes found an exit door, and he headed out at a dead run. Unfortunately, he exited into the corral that had been used for stagecoaches.

I calmly arose and walked across the front of the inn toward the corral. Well, I underestimated the cattle assassin.

McTavish turned out to be fleet afoot. He turned the opposite way from the direction I was approaching and vaulted over the corral fence. He dashed around the other side of the inn and made it to his horse. He mounted and spurred that cayuse to a dead run just as I doubled back in time to catch his triumphant gaze at me for having escaped my clutches.

Tornado was in the corral, so while I threw a saddle on him, McTavish was putting distance between us.

Once free of the corral, the pursuit was on. I picked up his horse's hoofprints right quickly. As luck would have it, McTavish's horse must have struck a rock and broken off part of the horseshoe on its right foreleg. That would make his tracks easier to distinguish and might eventually slow him down, depending on the terrain.

Now, Ambrose McTavish was traveling in my country. I knew most of the land around these parts like the back of my hand. I didn't figure him to get far before I caught up to him.

He left a track that a novice could follow. McTavish made his own path through the cenizo brush and thorny mesquite. So far as I could tell, he hadn't been wearing chaps, so the mesquite tore at his pants and shredded parts of his cape. Nevertheless, he had a good three-mile lead on me, and he eventually found a road.

It occurred to me that in addition to that menacing scythe, he might have a gun. Folks simply didn't ride around this part of Texas without one. He'd camped outside and ridden rough countryside enough that I had to believe that he was armed. If so, would he set an ambush? His style had been using that blade. I recalled how he'd killed cousin Nick's ranch hand with the scythe rather than shooting him. Was there some sort of message in that?

Assuming he had a gun, I had to move swiftly but cautiously. I tried to figure out where he might be heading. Thus far, he was heading northwest along the south bank of the Nueces River.

I followed for about five miles before his tracks turned and headed into the river. If he swam across, he could very well have been looking at me this very moment. I decided to stay put for a few minutes. If he was on the opposite shore and did have a gun, I'd be a sitting duck out there in the middle of the river.

I didn't have long to wait. I heard the faint sound of a horse's whinny and watched helplessly as I caught a brief image of McTavish heading southeast along the north bank of the Nueces River. I'd had to give him time to put some distance between us before I crossed.

McTavish's eastern direction got me to figuring the places he might be headed. With knowledge that he'd been in Beeville at least once, I had to consider that a possibility. He might even aim further south to Sinton or even do something bold like Corpus Christi. There were a lot of choices. He might even hop a train heading east. For now, I needed to close the gap so as to better figure out where he was ultimately headed.

I thought about Sheriff McTiernan, but if he showed up in Nuecestown, he hadn't a prayer of closing with me. I was on my own.

It finally occurred to me that Cassie would be wondering where I was or—worst case—what had befallen me. I decided that I'd best give her a call, if my situation afforded that opportunity.

McTavish's horse was still leaving tracks, though they'd be ever-more-difficult as the soil became sandier. There was plenty of scrub brush and pecan trees from which McTavish could set an ambush, but I sensed that he didn't have bushwhacking in mind yet—if at all. While he had some outdoor sense, I quickly realized that he hadn't a clue as to how to hide a trail. There was no evidence that he'd even attempted to backtrail to see whether I was following him.

It became clear that McTavish intended to skirt the north shore of Nueces Bay and head east toward Port Aransas. If he made it and could head north, his horse's hoofprints would be lost in the sand. I simply had to get close enough to see McTavish without him spotting me.

The land began to make a transition from plains to coastal prairies and marshes. Switchgrass would yield to saltgrass and gulf muhly. I was seeing ever-fewer mesquite trees, prickly pear cactus, and sage-like cenizo. Soon, live oak, hackberry, and many other indigenous trees were left behind me. As the sun dipped toward the horizon, I wondered whether McTavish dared stop for the night. The marshier terrain could get right dangerous for a rider unfamiliar with the territory. We'd been riding nonstop, and his horse must be as lathered as Tornado. I hoped and prayed that he'd decide to stop. If he did and laid low, he'd be like trying to find a needle in a haystack, given the darkness and foliage.

The setting sun was accompanied by a chill in the air. It was November, after all. Even McTavish wouldn't be fool enough to build a fire. Would he?

I'd guess that we'd made it to within five miles of Port Aransas. If his plan was to grab a train, he'd need to wait until daylight.

Now, here's where my familiarity with the terrain came into play. I knew a trail by which I was certain I could get in front of him. I could lay my own ambush to waylay the murderer.

Well, the devil be damned, I saw the telltale light of a fire off in the distance. Unless there were other travelers heading through these wide-open spaces, the fire had to have been set by McTavish. I guessed that the cold might have bested his common sense. Could he be thinking that he'd outrun me? Really?

McTavish was hungry. The scratches from mesquite, cactus, and other thorny vegetation had torn not only his clothes but his skin. The dropping temperature, along with a breeze across his sweaty duds, chilled him to the bone. Whatever critters were ranging around and yipping and howling in the brush made him uncomfortable, even with his trusty scythe by his side. He finally gathered some sticks and kindling and succumbed to building a fire. Being pursued hadn't been part of his plan.

Was someone still following him? That damned cowboy he'd seen in Nuecestown and later at the crossing of the Nueces River concerned him. Was it a lawman? He rejected that. There was no posse. All he'd read back east informed him that lawmen chasing lawbreakers always led a posse. Most importantly, was the man who'd set out after him still on his trail?

If he could make it to Post Aransas, he could grab a train out of South Texas. He could yet wreak his cattle carnage elsewhere. That thought brought him to considering what had become of Elder Barnabas. Had something happened to him? And what of his compatriots who were killing beeves in Colorado and Wyoming?

# FIFTEEN
# CAPTURE

I'D MANAGED to trace a wide path around what I assumed to be McTavish's fire. I ground-hitched Tornado, grabbed my Winchester, and began to stalk the murderer.

It was a slow slog. Even though I wasn't more than a couple of hundred yards away and downwind, there were marshy spots to avoid. There's little so annoying as stepping into a bog that nearly sucks your boot off. I came close a couple of times. My having hunted a few times around here was serving me in good stead. Now and then, I paused to listen. It's notable that at night, when you're striving to listen, there's a veritable cacophony of sounds from crickets, frogs, birds, and more. Fortunately, I hadn't stepped on any critters.

Well, I had gotten to within fifty feet when McTavish's horse began fidgeting around and whinnying. Damn! I watched McTavish awaken and stand with that damnable scythe in one hand and a gun in the other. With the bright glare of the fire, he was unable to see me beyond the circle of firelight. On the other hand, I could see him just fine. The next few minutes would be critical. I moved another ten feet closer. He still couldn't see me.

In the fire's glow, I made out the panic in the man's eyes. "Ambrose McTavish, you are under arrest. Drop your weapons and raise your hands over your head." I wasn't a lawman, of course, but he didn't know that.

He turned in my direction and strained to spot me beyond the fire.

"Drop those weapons," I warned again.

He raised the revolver and shot in my general direction. He wasn't much of a marksman, but I didn't want him to get lucky. Six shots. I heard the click on an empty cartridge. Unlike many of us who kept a chamber empty during travel to prevent any accidental self-inflicted wound, McTavish had fired a full load. He began fumbling to shake out the casings with the intention of reloading.

I aimed low with the Winchester. Forty feet was well within my range. I could shoot the eyes out of a running coyote at this distance, even in the dim light. I squeezed off a round that split McTavish's kneecap. He emitted a scream and fell, writhing in pain.

I took a couple more steps toward him only to see the scythe sweep the air above his prone body. McTavish was down but not out. I took careful aim and fired another shot in an attempt to hit the scythe. Naturally, I missed. The scythe was no running coyote. "Give it up, McTavish!" I commanded. "I don't want to kill you."

"You damned meat-eaters are going to die!" he hollered.

"Did Elder Barnabas tell you to die for vegetables, McTavish? Think about it. Use your head, man. Give it up." I tried to talk him into surrendering. Technically, I couldn't arrest him, but I could capture him and take him in. "Put down that scythe," I ordered.

"You busted my knee, you sonofabitch! You're one of

those damned ranchers raising cattle," he groaned. "Meat is the end of the world! It's the great sin! You're all of the devil!" McTavish sounded like some Bible-toting raving half-mad preacher, but he wasn't spouting biblical truths.

"Put down the scythe," I directed once again. I shook my head in dismay. How could anyone be so naïve, so unlearned as to fall for such claptrap? "I don't want to kill you, McTavish." Maybe a bullet through his other knee would bring him to his senses.

Using the scythe as a crutch, McTavish stood shakily, but his eyes breathed fire. Despite standing mostly on his one good leg, he whipped the scythe around as though it were some sort of medieval weapon. Little wonder that he was able to dispatch cattle with the terrible device. I dared not forget that he'd cut a cowboy in two. But for his shattered kneecap, he'd surely have run at me, wielding that wickedly evil instrument of death.

"Vegetarians for Life is gone, McTavish. They've arrested Elder Barnabas." I didn't know all this for a fact, but I didn't figure McTavish to know that. "It's over."

McTavish stood threateningly with fire in his eyes. "How can you eat meat?" he demanded. "It's an abomination. God didn't create man to be an eater of meat. It will be the end of the world!" I was expecting fire and brimstone to spew from his mouth.

Well, I'm no biblical scholar, but I knew his claim was untrue. "The Good Book doesn't say that at all, McTavish."

His knee oozed blood and sweat dripped from his brow despite the November chill. McTavish blinked. Had I struck some faint hint of common sense deep within the man?

Now, I'm not a Bible-toting believer, but sometimes things happen that transcend believability. As the wounded McTavish was standing there waving that damnable scythe at me, a pair of glowing eyes appeared in the firelight. A mountain lion had become brave and was sizing up McTavish as weak prey. I was downwind and likely obscured from the lion's view by McTavish himself. Mountain lions normally would avoid humans, but this one might have been weakened by wounds, was an old cat, or simply very hungry. "Don't move!" I commanded in a tone that would instantly freeze boiling water.

To his credit, McTavish froze.

I raised the Winchester and levered a round. I aimed just past McTavish and squeezed the trigger. The big cat took the bullet deep through his mouth and into his chest. He writhed, clawed the air, and then lay dying. His tail twitched for a few seconds before going limp.

A startled McTavish turned to see what I'd shot at. "Damn!" he exclaimed.

"There's meat that won't hurt you, McTavish," I said sarcastically.

"No!" he hollered. "You're lying!" Despite his knee, he lunged at me, sweeping the scythe before him. His leg collapsed, sending him crashing face-first into the ground, writhing in pain. The scythe flew free from his grasp and landed at my feet. McTavish, his face now covered in Texas bog, desperately tried to crawl toward the scythe. His knee simply wouldn't let him get that leg under him to leverage him toward me.

I clamped my foot down hard on the scythe snath. "Give it up, McTavish."

He reached a desperate clawing hand for the scythe.

"My God, man! Are you insane?" I whacked him up the side of his head with my rifle butt, and he fell back. McTavish lay still. I feared for a moment that I might have hit him hard enough to have killed him, but I'd merely knocked him out cold.

After knocking him out, I roped and hogtied him as any cowboy worth his salt would do. I didn't want him sneaking off in the night. I did have just enough compassion in me to clean his wounded knee as best I could. It didn't especially bother me to give him additional pain, as I poked and prodded it during the cleaning process. Fortunately, I did have some bandages in my saddlebags.

I skinned the mountain lion. I did see deep scars where the poor beast had been badly wounded. That might have accounted for his coming after human prey. I dragged the carcass far out into the brush as a gift to the coyotes.

Back in the camp, I examined McTavish's scythe closely. It was certainly no grass whipper. It had been fashioned as a weapon of death. The fine steel blade was attached to the handle by a locking device that enabled it to be securely stowed or opened for action. The highly polished snath itself was made from a wood I didn't recognize. I guessed ironwood, but there was none of that to be found around here. McTavish must have had the weapon custom-made back east.

I stoked the fire and took a nap, not waking until the sun painted the eastern sky with its golden fire.

Sufficiently rested come daylight, I warmed myself over the fire and packed up my prisoner. He was still groggy from that whack I'd given him. It wasn't until we were on the trail that McTavish finally came to. He was fit to be tied when he found his hands were tied behind him, and none too happy upon realizing that he was tied to the saddle of his horse. I had the bronc on a tether and was heading us toward Corpus Christi. I'd had the presence of mind to gag him, so I need not listen to any of his wild exhortations against eating meat. Elder Barnabas had sure found a true believer in Ambrose McTavish.

I rather chuckled to myself, as I thought on his ignominious end. There he rode, hogtied and still caked in Texas bog. His damp clothes made the November chill seem even colder. Discomfort was the least of his worries. McTiernan would arrest him for murder, and there was a fair chance he'd hang if he wasn't sentenced to live the rest of his life at the Texas State Prison in Huntsville. Every time I glanced back to check on my prisoner, he gave me a look that crossed between anger and insanity. He'd long ago transcended any pretense of being in his right mind.

It took a good part of the day to reach the north shore of Nueces Bay. I stopped and looked at the expanse of water ahead, then looked back at McTavish. His eyes said panic, especially as I headed Tornado into the water. McTavish hadn't a clue as to the existence of Reef Road. It was a formation of mostly oyster shells that wended its way between Nueces Bay and Corpus Christi Bay. At low tide, the water was only eighteen to twenty-four inches deep and was easily traversed by horseback or even wagons. In any case, McTavish hadn't a clue as to what lay ahead. He likely envisioned himself being swept helplessly from his horse and drowning. I can't say as I minded him having that fear.

Upon reaching the south shore of the bay, a diabolical thought occurred to me. Gagged and bound as he was, McTavish was my captive audience. I decided to extol the benefits of cattle and meat-eating. I drawled on as facts and stories came to me, turning in my saddle now and then to watch him seethe. We approached the outskirts of Corpus Christi as the sun began its fiery dance on the western horizon. I'd about run out of facts to annoy McTavish with, so the arrival was welcome.

I reined in and pulled McTavish's bronc alongside. He

was a sorry sight to see and stunk to high heaven. He'd peed himself along the way, as he was unable to call out to me about answering nature's call. He sure didn't resemble any stalwart crusader for vegetarians. I looked over and gave him my best condescending smile. I'd won, and he'd lost. "You ever consider that the horse you're riding is considered a delicacy in some places?" It was sort of my final teasing jab at the sonofabitch.

McTavish managed a growl through the gag. He tried to kick his horse into moving away, but I had a firm grip on the bridle.

"Let's go see Sheriff McTiernan," I finally stated and headed us toward the jail. The daylight was beginning to dim as we pulled up in front of McTiernan's office. A brass kerosene lamp flickered beside the door. Electricity hadn't overtaken all the lighting just yet. While it might have been unseemly to some, I decided to draw attention the old cowboy way. I pulled out my Smith & Wesson and pointed it to the sky. The shot echoed off buildings up and down the street.

Sheriff McTiernan came blasting through the doorway. "What in tarnation!" he shouted. In a single sweeping glance, he saw me and my prisoner. "Damn, Junior! You got him!"

There was no question as to whom I had in tow.

McTavish sat glowering from the saddle.

"Sheriff McTiernan, it's my pleasure to introduce Mr. Ambrose McTavish. He's come here to be placed under arrest for murder and damage to private property." I smiled triumphantly. "Looks as though he's been left speechless, Sheriff," I added.

"Damn, Junior. You could have cleaned him up a little before you brought him here. He needs a bath," said McTiernan.

"No problem, Sheriff." I untied McTavish's legs and yanked him down from his saddle. He tried to scream with pain despite the gag and staggered along owing to his broken kneecap. I leaned him against the hitching rail, then strode over to a nearby horse trough, scooped a bucket of water, and gave McTavish a good dousing. He sputtered as much as his gag would permit and gave me an even angrier glare, if that was possible. "There you go, Sheriff. He's all clean and pretty."

McTiernan stepped forward and looked in the prisoner's eyes. "Ambrose McTavish, I hereby place you under arrest for murder."

"He may need a doc for that knee, Sheriff." I tried not to be totally heartless. I finally faced McTavish. I untied the gag from his mouth. "Don't say a damned word, McTavish. Your days of killing cattle and taking a human life are over. I can only hope and pray they feed you beef all your days in prison. And, if you hang, may the Devil feed you beef for eternity." I turned and nodded to McTiernan. "He's all yours, Sheriff." At that, I headed off to find a room at the hotel.

Admittedly, I was feeling pretty doggone good about myself. I decided that I'd spend a few more dollars of the expenses associated with my pursuit of Ambrose McTavish for some personal comfort. Kleberg could afford it. I set my sights on the Hotel Alexander, the finest hotel in Corpus Christi. It sat overlooking the bay. I featured myself enjoying a glass of wine while contemplating the view from the balcony of one of their best suites. A fine evening was surely overdue, especially after the day's events.

My first order of business upon reaching the hotel was to call Cassie and let her know that I was okay and had brought McTavish to justice. My second call was to Archer Parr. I looked forward to that second five thousand dollars being deposited in the Corpus Christi National Bank. I had some thoughts as to what I might do with that money.

I checked into the hotel and agreed that it was indeed the best Corpus Christi had to offer, set as it was near a salt cedar grove that provided shaded outdoor spaces and featured a bayfront location that afforded access to bathing, fishing, and boating. Importantly, I ordered a bath that I so desperately sought. Corpus Christi had a city water system for nearly a decade now, so filling a tub was easy enough. Heating was more of a challenge, but doable.

While waiting for the tub to fill, I called Cassie to share the good news.

"Hello?" she answered the telephone noncommittedly. That was usually the case when we didn't know who was calling. The operator hadn't alerted her.

"Sweetheart, it's me. I captured McTavish and turned him over to Sheriff McTiernan."

"Lucas? Are you heading home? It's awful dark."

"I'm spending the night at the Hotel Alexander. I'll be home in the morning."

"Congratulations, my love. I'll cook up something special," she promised.

"Love you. See you tomorrow." I hung up.

A uniformed porter was adding hot water to my bath. Warm towels had been set on a table to one side. I reckoned that there was time to call Parr.

"Archer? It's me, Lucas Dunn," I announced.

"Junior? Did you get him?" Parr asked right away. There was no *how are you* or *are you okay*.

"He's sitting in McTiernan's jail."

"Good job, Junior," he stated. "You okay?"

I appreciated that he'd asked. "I'm good. McTavish not so much. He's got a busted knee for his trouble."

Parr laughed. "Glad it's over. We'll keep our end up, if you know what I mean?"

"Thanks kindly, Archer," I responded.

"Come visit sometime," he said and hung up.

I wondered what his invite was about, but the bath beckoned. I slipped into the warm water and truly relaxed. I let its eddies soothe my tired bones as I immersed myself. I came back up sputtering a bit. Oh, but it felt so good.

The pursuit of McTavish had been quite a test, so I looked forward to focusing on ranching and the chores that kept us busy through the South Texas winter. I suppose that could be described as returning to normal. I had plenty of time to consider any future undertakings.

I poured a glass of wine and let the waters penetrate my pores, into the very depths of my body. I closed my eyes and sank back into the depths as far as my six-foot-three frame would permit. As I closed my eyes to more fully be absorbed in relaxation, I was jolted to attention.

Two soft white hands caressed my shoulders. The sweet aroma of perfume hung in the air.

"Hi, cowboy," she cooed, as she breathed softly on my neck, pressed her breasts against me, and let her curls fall beside my head.

I instantly stood. Buck-naked and dripping wet, I found myself facing a barely clothed seductress. Her long red hair fell in graceful waves across her ample chest. Her eyes? Well, her eyes were focused on my manhood, exposed for all the world to see. I grabbed a towel and covered myself. "What the hell are you doing here?" I demanded.

"The porter left the door open, so I came in. I didn't mean to startle you, sir." She was now nearly as embarrassed as me. It seemed that leaving the guest's door ajar when a bath had been drawn had become a signal for any adventurous soiled dove.

I'd gathered my wits by now. I had to admit; she was far too beautiful to be in the prostitution business. "Well, there's been a mistake, darlin'. You run along." I reached over to my pants hanging on the bedpost and fetched out a silver dollar. I gave it to her and hustled her out the door, closing it solidly behind her. I dropped the towel and glanced down. Yes, she was arousal material.

How was it that I seemed to attract women hell-bent on using their enticing charms to bed me? To my credit, fending off those charmers was made easier for me, given that I could come home to my beautiful and exceedingly seductive wife. Then again, Cassie was blessed to have a man who was committed to her and her alone.

I toweled off and slipped into a robe. The chill that hit me, as I walked onto the balcony was refreshing. I raised my glass as a toast to the lights of Corpus Christi spread before me. It had surely been a good day.

My stomach growled. I was hungry. I dressed and headed to the hotel dining room, where I reckoned to enjoy a luscious, rarely-cooked steak with all the fixings. Once dinner was placed in front of me, I had a momentary urge to go eat it at the jail in front of McTavish.

Upon exiting the hotel, I encountered the young lady who had intended to make my bath a special experience. She gave a sweet smile and a little wave as she finished business with the man standing before her. She stuffed something between her breasts, then pivoted and walked off. I couldn't help but appreciate the provocative wiggle of her posterior as she walked away. She gave a little peek over her shoulder to see whether I was watching. I was.

At the stable, I saddled Tornado. "We're headed home, Tornado. We can get back to ranching," I said to my four-legged companion. I rolled up the mountain lion skin and tied it behind the saddle. I figured it would make a nice wall decoration in the study I decided to add to the house.

Frost covered the landscape as I headed Tornado toward Heaven's Gate Ranch. My libido had been challenged, and I yearned for Cassie. There was something about homecomings that were special. I chuckled to myself. Going home was more than about good grub.

# SIXTEEN
# OPPORTUNITY

BEFORE I KNEW IT, the new year had arrived. It was a time for reflection. What would 1901 bring? I didn't have to wait long.

Cassie and I sat at breakfast in mid-January. It had actually snowed the previous day, leaving a coating of a couple of inches of white across the landscape. The livestock took it in stride, but the kids and dogs loved the frosty stuff. We even made a snowman with a cowboy hat and a carrot nose.

So, we sat there sipping coffee and reading the Corpus Christi Caller Times. I'd divided the paper into two so Cassie could enjoy part of it. Sean and Bode played in the corner of the kitchen, while little Carolyn toddled around with her first steps.

"Cassie, listen to this!" I announced. "Some oil well over in Beaumont that they call Spindletop blew oil a few days ago. It was what they call a gusher, sweetheart. It's apparently taken their best efforts to cap the well. The article claims it's the biggest gusher in the country."

"Does it mean anything for us, Lucas?" She squinted at

me as though asking whether I had some plan in mind. Cassie read me like a book; a well-read book.

I nonchalantly sipped some coffee. "I've been at those wells up in Corsicana. Beamont isn't all that far from there."

She gave me that *so-what-are-you-planning* sort of look as she tried to calmly take a sip of her own coffee.

"I've a mind to use some of those ten thousand dollars from Parr to invest in oil. Why not an oil well right here at Heaven's Gate Ranch? There's a tar bog at the far end of our ranch. I'd bet that patch is full of oil." There, I'd said it.

Cassie looked apprehensive. In her mind, the money was insurance against hard times.

"Texas is going to be crawling with speculators, oil companies, and the hangers-on that accompany any boom, whether it be gold, silver, or oil. Spindletop is only the beginning." I could see that she wasn't convinced. "Tell you what; I won't invest more than five thousand dollars."

She placed her coffee cup gently on the table before her and looked across at me. Exploring for oil sounded far safer than being a lawman. She gracefully arose from the chair and glided over to me with a smile beginning to find its way across her face. She eased onto my lap, wrapped her arms around me, and planted a heaven-sent kiss that devoured my lips. "I love you. Go have fun with your oil adventure." Her hand slipped inside my shirt and caressed my chest. "The children are napping," she sighed, pressing herself against me.

I needed no further encouragement. The bearskin rug in front of the hearth with its invitingly-warm fire called out to me. Tangling with Cassie and her passions on a bearskin rug was a heavenly delight. From her moans and sighs, there was no doubt that the feelings were mutual. Her magical hands did things to me that transcended intimacy. Damn, but I was a lucky man!

Oil! I had managed to learn a bit about the so-called black gold business during my pursuit of the Irish Mob. If I were to finance an oil well at Heaven's Gate Ranch, where might it be best located? I recalled an area at the far southeastern boundary that we'd written off years ago as a bog. However, it wasn't like the bogs to be found around places like Aransas Pass or farther to the south around Los Olmos. I recalled that there was a bit of sticky black substance mixed in. We fenced it off to keep the cattle away from it. Now, it occurred to me that the black stuff was tar. There wasn't a lot of it, but it could very well mean that oil lurked beneath the surface. If my hunch was right, our investment in a well might spell security for Dunn generations to come. It entailed risk.

To put this oil venture in perspective, I never looked at money as an end in itself. We needed enough to live with reasonable comfort and run the ranch. My dad taught me that the worship of money was evil, as it took over men's minds and often led them to do evil things. As a lawman, I'd seen money worship. Greed was its prime manifestation. Folks obsessed with acquiring wealth believe that having ever more money will lead to greater happiness. Ironically, they will never have enough money to meet their desires.

Well, we'd see about the wealth end of the oil business. Meanwhile, the case with the Irish Mob had connected me with the Railroad Commission of Texas, thanks to Archer Parr's connection with its chairman, John Reagan. The Commission lacked direct power over the oil-industry, but I reckoned that the oil boom likely to follow the Spindletop gusher would quickly increase rail traffic, as crude oil, drilling equipment, and workers would be moved by rail.

The Commission's existing rate-setting and safety rules for railroads therefore indirectly affected the oil business by governing how oil was transported. It was an incremental step toward control. However, there were no regulations just yet. The time was opportune for my venture in pursuit of black gold.

I saw oil as representing the ultimate taming of the Texas frontier. The land had absorbed the blood, sweat, and tears of the men and women who'd striven to tame it. Red, Black, Brown, White—skin color didn't matter to the soil that was Texas. Cattle and cotton had been economic royalty, but they scratched the surface. Oil gushing from deep within the bowels of the land would become king. Black gold would rule.

With winter upon us and the apocalyptic ghost of Ambrose McTavish behind me, I could focus full bore on drilling for oil. I was comfortable with purchasing all the equipment and supplies needed, but more importantly, I had to lure an experienced crew to the ranch. I reckoned a little journey up to Corsicana was in my future.

While I was anxious to jump into drilling, I knew that there was plenty to do before a drill bit broke the earth. I decided that I'd wait until March to head to Corsicana to recruit an oil rig crew. It seemed to make sense that there'd be an overabundance of labor as a consequence of men coming in following the announcement of the Spindletop gusher. The more laborers available, the less I'd have to pay. That was simply a law of economics that I'd learned in the cattle business. Abundant supply translated to lower prices, while lower supply creates demand and higher prices.

# SEVENTEEN
# ESCAPE!

FEBRUARY WAS a tad tough in South Texas. The temperatures hovered at or barely above freezing from sunup to sundown. I found myself thawing out one afternoon in my favorite chair near the fireplace when the telephone rang. That infernal device would surely become the bane of most folks' existence, especially as it insisted on being answered. Cassie was busy with baby Carolyn upstairs, so answering was up to me.

I lifted myself up and headed to the telephone. "Hello? Luke Dunn here," I greeted.

"Luke? McTiernan here." The sheriff sounded panicky. He breathed heavily. "McTavish escaped!"

"What?" he exclaimed.

"They were transporting him to prison in Huntsville. The wagon broke down, and he escaped."

"Are they chasing him?" I asked, as the reality sank in. Would McTavish be the vengeful type?

"Far as I can tell. He won't be running after you ruined his knee," replied McTiernan.

"Where'd he make his escape?" I pressed.

"They were transporting him to catch a train in Victoria. He escaped near Beeville," McTiernan paused. "I know what this means to you, Junior. If you must chase him, I'll consider you deputized. But consider that he took weapons and money from the guards. He killed one and wounded another." McTiernan knew that he was offering me a license to kill, along with a solid reason.

I thought on it. I'd promised Cassie that I wouldn't pin on the Texas Ranger badge. The devil is in the distinction. Would it be okay if I only used the badge as cover for bringing justice to McTavish? But for the telephone being linked to the wall, I'd already be out the door and heading for Beeville. "Okay, John. I'm going after him."

We said our goodbyes, and, just as I hung up, I found Cassie standing inches from me.

"Going after whom, Lucas Dunn?" she challenged.

"McTavish escaped," I announced. "I must ride. He's around Beeville."

Cassie gave me her suspicious look. "He deputized you, didn't he," she stated factually.

I nodded.

"Go, Lucas. Do what you must," she kissed me and handed me my buffalo skin coat. "You'll need this."

While I headed to saddle Tornado, Cassie put together grub for my hunt. She wouldn't want her man to go hungry, even though he'd broken his vow—at least in her mind.

I became more alert as I entered Bee County. Had McTavish found transportation? He'd have a tough go of it on foot. The winter cold and his ruined knee would make for slow going. To make matters a tad more challenging, there was an inch or so of snow coating the landscape.

I reckoned that my first stop in Beeville would be familiar ground to McTavish. Schilo's Saloon beckoned in the fading daylight. Would McTavish dare stop there? I took a long, appraising look at the saloon. It was a cold night. There were no horses hitched in front of the place. I decided to stable Tornado and grab a room at the Commercial Hotel before heading to Schilo's to grab dinner and possibly learn something about my prey. Prey he was. There was no forgiveness in me. I was the hunter, and he was the hunted.

I stabled Tornado and headed to the hotel.

"Howdy, Mr. Dunn," greeted the hotel desk clerk. "Good to have you visit us again." He grabbed a room key and even signed me in. "May I assist you with anything?" He'd noted my usual luggage: saddlebags and rifle.

"I'm heading to Schilo's to grab some grub. Any chance you've seen a man with his left leg pretty much crippled?"

"There was a man with a terrible limp, took a room here last night. He was looking for a horse. Not many for sale around here this time of year."

"What was he wearing?" I asked.

"He wore a heavy coat. I couldn't see what he wore under it, Mr. Dunn." The clerk rubbed his chin in thought, then had a eureka moment. "His pants might have been striped when he checked in, but when he went to breakfast this morning at Schilo's, he was dressed pretty regular."

"Any idea where he is now?"

"Never returned from Schilo's," responded the clerk.

"Will you show me his room?" I asked.

"Sure." The clerk grabbed a key and led me up the hallway. He knocked on the door, but there was no answer.

"Open it," I requested.

The hotel clerk unlocked the door and swung it open for

me to enter. It opened only halfway, as it butted against what appeared to be a body lying on the floor. Well, that's exactly what it was.

"Oh my God!" hollered the clerk. "That's Mr. Terwilliger!"

I was something less than surprised. McTavish was obviously desperate. "This is how your guest got rid of his striped clothes." I kneeled down and felt for a pulse but had already figured the man to be dead. "You keep it quiet, son, but fetch the sheriff. I'm heading to Schilo's," I directed him. I sensed that McTavish just might be there.

The clerk's jaw gaped with surprise, as I went to step past him. He began to point, but was speechless with fear. His hand trembled.

I had looked down briefly to avoid stepping on Terwilliger's body. As my head came up, I couldn't miss the clerk's eyes looking past me in horror.

"Th…there!" he finally managed a warning. He pointed behind me.

This maneuvering was all occurring in split seconds. I spun and leaped sideways in a single motion just as a bullet buzzed past my head. There was McTavish, holding a smoking revolver. Down on one knee, I ducked lower and drew my Smith & Wesson.

McTavish, flush with rage, fired another shot and missed again. I aimed carefully and placed a .38 caliber slug into his throat just below his jaw. He went rigid for a moment, eyes wide. In that split second, he must have realized that all the beef in the world wasn't worth this price. The pause was enough for me to put a second round into his chest. McTavish was dead before he hit the floor. The world wouldn't end, but he had.

I heard a groan behind me and turned to see the hotel desk clerk sitting on the floor with a flesh wound along the side of his head. There was a lot of blood but little damage. "You okay, son?" I asked.

"I think I'm dying," he lamented pitifully.

"You're going to live. The doc will have you patched up in no time." I handed him a towel to staunch the bleeding. "You stay here and guard these bodies while I go find the sheriff."

I dusted myself off and headed out to find Sheriff Fuller. As I headed past the bodies, I thought on McTavish's end. He'd fancied himself the pale horseman of the apocalypse, the deliverer of death. But justice defied death. Evil had been defeated. Still, I wished I could have captured him again. I found it ever-tougher to accommodate killing anyone.

Upon exiting the front door of the hotel, I scanned up and down the street. The hotel had muffled the sounds of the shooting, so no crowd was forming. I was heading toward the jail, when I nearly walked headlong into the sheriff.

"Whoa! What's the hurry?" asked Fuller.

"Been a killing at the Commercial, Sheriff," I responded.

"Who the hell are you?" he naturally asked, as he headed past me on a fast walk to the hotel.

"I'm Luke Dunn, one of Sheriff McTiernan's deputies out of Nueces County," I replied, near breathless as I chugged along behind him. My own tiredness, coupled with the stress of the gunfight with McTavish, had me breathing hard.

"I know McTiernan," he allowed, as we climbed the steps to the Commercial Hotel. He paused before heading upstairs. "Your father was a Texas Ranger, wasn't he? You too." He headed up the stairs with me right behind him. "What am I going to find?" he finally asked.

"Two bodies, Sheriff," I replied.

"Dead, I presume?" he queried sort of rhetorically.

We were soon standing over the bodies. The desk clerk still sat by the bed with the blood-stained towel against the side of his head.

I pointed to McTavish. "This one is Ambrose McTavish. He escaped while being transported to Huntsville. He shot at me, so I returned fire," I described my role succinctly and matter-of-factly. "Apparently, he killed Terwilliger there to steal the man's clothes."

Fuller looked at the clerk. "You witness this, Freddy?"

"It be as he said, Sheriff," he moaned. "Can I go see the doc?"

"Looks like you're clean, Dunn," observed Fuller. "I'd be grateful if you'd write this up and leave it at my office in the morning." He turned to the clerk. "Freddy, after you see the doc, get Slim and Johnny to lug McTavish off to Boot Hill. Store Terwilliger in the cold locker until we can notify kinfolk."

It hit me that I was hungry and tired. "You need any more from me, Sheriff?"

"You look tired, Dunn. Thanks for dealing with this threat. I'll let you know, if I need anything else."

I left Fuller at the scene and headed over to Schilo's to grab a bite. I can't describe my feelings as relaxed or even relieved, but the tenseness within me had mostly subsided. It seemed strange that on the heels of having killed a man I could eat. Had I become numbed to taking lives? Was it the lawman in me? I'd surely have much preferred capturing McTavish. As I thought back, I had killed only one man, Kyle McClintock, for whom I had a personal grudge underlying my lawman duties. No, it was essentially an unpleasant byproduct of the job.

I was soon sitting at Schilo's Saloon with a half-eaten steak sitting in front of me. It was downright delicious.

Then it hit me. It wasn't that I killed McTavish. Nope. Two bullets had been fired at me with the intention of taking my life. I wasn't even a Texas Ranger anymore. Damn, but I seemed to be leading a charmed life.

I left my steak unfinished and headed for my room at the hotel. I sat on the bed but fell back and was asleep before I could even shed my boots.

Next morning, I called Cassie to let her know that I was all right and McTavish had been disposed of. Then, I called McTiernan to let him know what happened. He backed my deputization with Sheriff Fuller to ensure that I wasn't held for killing McTavish. It was but a small detail that I was out of his jurisdiction, but the folks in Beeville were relieved to be rid of McTavish. I managed to write a description of what had happened at the hotel and left it at Fuller's office.

The clerk sported a nasty headache and a bandage wrapped around his head like some badge of honor. He now had an exciting story to share with family and friends. The Commercial Hotel didn't charge me for the night's stay. That was right nice of them.

I grabbed breakfast at Schilo's Saloon and headed home none the worse for wear. I could finally fully relax about McTavish and focus on my oil venture.

# EIGHTEEN
# NOT SO EASY

IT WAS great to be home. I received an appreciative letter from the Office of the Governor for my role in bringing McTavish to justice. Kleberg and Parr were certainly grateful, and the ranchers in the region just about fell all over themselves with gratitude. I suppose it could be said that I'd made a name for myself, perhaps even rivaling my legendary dad.

Of course, I could never really compare with my dad. He was of another era. An Irish emigrant, he had begun life in America working security for Corpus Christi founder Colonel Kinney's cock fights before joining the Texas Rangers. He chased down killers, became close friends with a couple of savage Comanche chiefs, rooted out government fraud, and dealt with the times of the War Between the States and its aftermath. That had been more than a war. It had been a national tragedy of epic proportions, though it also cleansed the nation's soul. It had been a war of kin against kin; flags rising and flags falling.

Dad never saw a battle line. He fought to keep the law in South Texas, fending off deserters and foragers alike. He and Mom managed to raise ten children and build Heaven's Gate Ranch into one of the biggest in Texas. He was a legend, a tough act to follow. But I really wasn't trying. I became my own man. This was a different time with different problems. My destiny began when I faced down that bully years ago in Corpus Christi. I suppose you could say my dad's era was pre-oil and mine was post-oil. Of course, that was far too simple. Droves of settlers and the railroads had indeed radically changed the cultural and economic landscape. And now, I was about to launch into the oil business.

Unsurprisingly, Captain Hughes had heard of my exploits with the cattle killer and reached out to ask whether I was ready to join him in fighting rebellious Mexicans and ornery Apache renegades along the Rio Grande. The political machinations of President Diaz seemed to be stirring things up south of the border. I turned him down, much to Cassie's pleasure. I was amply rewarded in our bed that night.

A concerning surprise arrived in the mail one day toward the end of February. Cassie saw that it was addressed to me, so left it on the table in our foyer. The envelope was made from an unusual, bright yellow paper. It was as though the sender didn't want it to be missed. As I walked in that afternoon from checking beeves most of the day, it immediately caught my eye. Upon examining it, I noted that there was no return address on the envelope. I was going to have to open it to find whom it was from.

My Bowie knife would have been overkill to slit open the envelope, so I used a nearby letter opener to cut the seal. I was a tad clumsy, as I hadn't removed my gloves. I fumbled a bit, but managed to part the opening and peek inside.

Now, here's where chance plays in our lives. Inside the envelope was a white powdery substance. I wasn't able to tell what it was by looking at it, and I surely wasn't about to touch it, taste it, or smell it. The word *DIE* was scrawled in bold black letters inside the flap of the envelope. The substance was likely poison. Thank God I kept my gloves on and hadn't sneezed or—God forbid—stuck my nose into the envelope. From what little I knew of poisons, this was probably strychnine. It was powerful. Who would be trying to poison me and why?

I didn't reckon this to be Sheriff McTiernan's field of expertise. He was more a political animal without the clout to interact with larger law enforcement organizations that possessed greater evidentiary resources. Maybe, Archer Parr knew someone who could resolve this macabre effort to kill me.

As I headed to the telephone, Cassie intercepted me. "Who was that letter from, Lucas?" she asked innocently. She reached out to welcome me home, but I stepped back and raised my gloved hands with the envelope still in my grasp. I held it tightly closed.

I figured it best to get the truth of the threat out in the open right off. "Don't touch it or my gloves. It likely contains strychnine. Someone is trying to poison me."

She stood back with mouth agape. "But, who?" she gasped.

"Good question. I'm fixing to give Archer Parr a holler. He may have the contacts to find out." It occurred to me that the envelope and gloves posed an immediate danger to my family as well as me. "Let me put these out of harm's way first." I nodded toward the door, and Cassie opened it to let me out. "Grab a shovel and dig a shallow hole for now, and we'll temporarily bury the envelope and my gloves. We may need them later for evidence."

Cassie dug a shallow hole and lined it with a towel upon which I carefully placed the envelope and my gloves.

I closed the towel over them and backfilled the hole. With temporary disposal accomplished, we went back inside, and I called Parr.

"Archer? It's Luke Dunn."

"I know it's you, Junior. The operator said you were calling," chuckled Parr.

I kept forgetting that operators out here would often announce callers. "I have a big problem," I said with a deeply concerned tone.

"What's up?" Parr asked with feigned concern.

"I just received an anonymous bright yellow envelope containing poison."

Silence.

"Did you hear me?" I pressed.

"Who would want to do a thing like that, Junior?" queried Parr.

"That's what I'm hoping you might help me with. Who wants me dead? Who would be so diabolical as to endanger my family? What if Cassie had opened the envelope?"

"Let me call a couple of folks who may shed some light. It's a chance, Junior. This sort of thing is beyond local concern. I'll get back to you as soon as I learn something."

"Thanks, Archer," I said and hung up. For better or worse, I sure was developing a working relationship with the man.

I awakened next morning to a telephone call from Parr. This would be interesting. By now, the news that someone had tried to poison Luke Dunn would be spreading all over South Texas thanks to the party line telephone system. It was one of the hazards folks had to deal with. So be it.

"Luke, can you get over here to San Diego? I can't talk about this on the telephone. Too many ears."

"Be there in a couple of hours," I responded and hung up.

Cassie awakened. "Important?" she asked groggily.

"Parr has something. I need to go to San Diego." I got dressed quickly. As I dashed out the door, Cassie put a cup of hot coffee in my hands and a couple of warm biscuits. They'd have to suffice as breakfast, as I headed to the barn to saddle up Tornado.

☆☆

It was around ten o'clock, when I knocked at Parr's office.

Parr opened the door and motioned me to enter. His office assistant, an attractive young lady, smiled knowingly as we went to Parr's office and shut the door. Did everyone know what was happening?

"Sit, Junior. First off, everything is under control." With that opening statement, he poured us each a cup of coffee.

"Under control?" I asked. Had something been out of control?

"Rudy Kleberg said that he's ninety-nine percent certain that the envelope was sent by Elder Barnabas of that Vegetarians for Life cult. He was being questioned by police in Washington, and they told him you'd killed Ambrose McTavish. Turns out that the news angered him more than he let on in the interview. The interrogators left him unattended for a few moments, and he escaped. This was two weeks ago, so it would have given him time to obtain the poison and send it to you. He certainly had motive and, from what Rudy says, had the means. It turns out that the cult had used strychnine in some of its cattle killings. Elder Barnabas even had bright yellow stationery in his office. It's circumstantial but damning nonetheless."

I sat there pretty much stunned. "Who'd have reckoned them to be that psychotic?" I finally blurted rhetorically.

Parr took a sip of coffee. He looked at the contents. "Yuck. Who brewed this swill?" Turned out to be left over from the previous day. He shook off the distraction and turned back to me. "Elder Barnabas is back in police custody. They coaxed a confession from him. They'll charge him with attempted murder, so that should have him out of commission and of no further danger to you or your family."

"I appreciate you resolving this, Archer," I said gratefully. "Guess we can rest easy."

"You can understand why I didn't want to say anything over the telephone. Doggone, but those things can sprout ears." He gave another one of his easy chuckles.

"I'll be headed to Corsicana in a couple of weeks. I'll look up those folks you mentioned."

"I think you just might succeed, Junior," he responded earnestly.

"Thanks. I'll get out of your hair and be heading home." With that, I departed. As I strode past the young lady, I put my fingers to my lips as though to imply silence.

She nodded. "We keep a lot of secrets here, Mr. Dunn."

I can't say that didn't surprise me.

March seemed to take forever to roll around. I guess time seemed to take longer to pass, because I was excited to begin our oil venture. I had accumulated the equipment and supplies I would need to begin drilling operations and stored them all near that tar-laden bog on the far reaches of the ranch. I only lacked labor, especially a knowledgeable foreman.

While on the Irish Mob case, I had learned and then observed how oil drilling began with a derrick. It housed the drilling equipment and was essential for lifting the heavy drill bits and casing pipes that were part of the process. I reckoned to use a rotary drill bit like the one employed at Spindletop. Drilling for oil was a laborious process fraught with danger. What they called drilling mud, comprised of clay and water, would be used to cool the drill bit, remove debris, and stabilize the wellbore. The casing pipes would be used to stabilize drilling challenges beneath the derrick, such as quicksand and unstable formations. The Spindletop well had drilled to a depth of around a thousand feet before striking oil. I figured that we'd drill down at least that far. We might find oil, but it could be a dry hole. That was the risk we took in putting our money and resources into this effort.

I considered it a special blessing that the oil business was new to Texas. There were rumblings of oversight from the Railroad Commission of Texas, but nothing formal forthcoming. I knew intuitively that once the government stuck its hands in the oil trough, regulations would abound and only wealthy financiers would thrive. My earnest hope was to be ahead of that eventuality, as small-time entrepreneurs like myself would be priced out. I was not a fan of government regulation, as it could become so burdensome that it choked off freedom. That having been said, some regulation was needed, from protecting laborers to ensuring fair business practices. I welcomed and dreaded that reality. The timing, in my humble judgment, could hardly be better.

For now, economies of scale alone would contribute toward dictating winners and losers, not to mention the risk of actually finding oil. The dry hole lurked as a distinct possibility. The more holes that could be drilled in promising terrain, the greater the chances of success.

I sat staring into my coffee. "Tomorrow," I replied in answer to Cassie's question about when I'd be heading to Corsicana. I'd heard that plenty of laborers were available. I had to recruit a foreman first and foremost. Such a man would then select the drillers, derrickmen, roughnecks, tool pushers, and mechanics essential to the drilling. I would also need teamsters with tankers to transport the much-anticipated oil to a refinery.

"When will we begin drilling?" she asked.

"When I get the men hired and on the site." It was a perfunctory response, and Cassie had known the answer before she asked the question. I must have answered it twenty times over the past couple of months. I suppose part of it was that I'd become so immersed in the oil business that I wasn't quite so devoted to her, home, and our ranch. Was oil becoming my mistress? It had better not. I looked across the kitchen table at my beautiful, loving wife. "I'm sorry, Cassie. I guess I've been too wrapped up in this oil thing."

She smiled sweetly and sipped her coffee. "Really," she replied with gentle sarcasm.

Oh, how right she was. Even our romps in bed had become infected by my thoughts about oil. "Yes. I truly am."

"Your children will become strangers if you keep this up, Lucas Dunn."

When she used my full name, it didn't bode well. I reckoned I'd better straighten up and set things right. "We're invested in this, and I fear failure." There, I'd admitted it. I could handle a dry hole, but to invest so much and not give it the best chance for success would be failure.

"Oh, Lucas. I wouldn't love you any less." She arose and refilled our coffee cups, then sat back down beside me. "You must never fear failure. By trying, you're far above those who've never tried, so will never know success or failure. That spirit is a part of you that I treasure. You've always found a way to provide for us, Lucas." Cassie gave me an especially loving look. "But, never let pursuit of success cost you the ones you love."

My mom couldn't have said it better. In fact, it's what she would have said and surely advised my dad of the same. Cassie supported everything I did, even my days as a Texas Ranger, where death could grab my reins at any turn on the trail. "I understand, sweetheart. I love you and the kids more than life itself."

Her arm slipped around me, and she nibbled my ear. "We have some business on that bearskin rug to tend to before you ride off to Corsicana."

That bearskin rug was going to get worn out, or so I hoped. Fur sure has a way of bringing out the animal in folks engaging in carnal pursuits.

☆☆

As I prepared to head to Corsicana, there were plenty of chores to do. A ranch owner worth his salt didn't let his ranch hands do all the work. I carried my share of fence repairs, stall mucking, and the like.

With the warmer weather, all sorts of critters began emerging from nooks and crannies around the ranch. Predators began their hunts for prey while scavengers undertook their ritualistic hovering to get to any leftovers. Deer, javelina, rabbits, prairie dogs—the prey the predators sought—enjoyed the fresh green shoots of grasses. Birds sang and began building nests, while the landscape was enveloped in a cover of green as buds filled the trees. One of the less desirable emergences was the ever-present rattlesnake. An old cowboy saying was that a tough man would take on a nest of rattlers and spot them the first bite. Well, bitten was a decidedly undesirable outcome. Everyone around the ranch kept their eyes peeled for those slinking, poisonous serpents. Carelessness was not an option.

One morning, I decided to saddle Tornado and take a ride. Well, as I entered the barn, I heard the telltale buzz of a rattler vibrating those rattles gracing the end of its tail. Around these parts, the natural reaction would be to step away from that buzz. Believe me, I would have if I could have. A second rattler kicked up a rattle just a few feet behind me. Now, I was being serenaded by a duet of the deadly reptiles. These were big as rattlers go. They were both better than five feet long and weren't starving. They were obviously successful in keeping down the vermin population around the ranch. Well, I wasn't vermin, and I was facing a bit of a problem.

What happened next was measured in fractions of seconds. Normally, I'd have slipped my Smith & Wesson from my holster and blown the threatening serpent away. With two of them, that was no longer an option. Shooting one would likely cause the other to strike. I wasn't about to have those twin fangs inject the rattler's venom into me. I jumped forward. Both rattlers lunged! Blessedly, they struck thin air. However, that wasn't the end of it. They writhed for a moment on the dusty floor of the barn to gather themselves for another try.

While they were busy coiling themselves for another attack, I drew my revolver. At six feet or so range, hitting what you point your gun at isn't called aiming. Lord knows, I'd shot enough rattlesnakes—and a couple of water moccasins—through their heads without half trying at twice the distance. Two shots echoed through the barn, and two rattlers lay dead. Not bad for a morning's work.

Where there were two rattlesnakes, I reckoned there'd be more. A nest was likely to be nearby. Jake had proven adept at finding the nests, so I made a note to myself to get him to eliminate the one that spawned the two I'd just dispatched.

I was about to hang the carcasses over a railing as a reminder when it occurred to me that they were right good eating. I drew out my Bowie knife and carefully chopped off the heads of both snakes. Even the fangs of a dead rattlesnake can have enough residual venom to make a man mighty ill if a fang snagged his skin. I headed back to the house with decapitated reptiles slung over my shoulder.

Cassie didn't flinch. She knew just how to cook the rattlers. That's the way it was with women on Texas ranches. Fried rattlesnake would be featured on this evening's menu.

With the snakes in Cassie's capable hands, I took my ride on Tornado. I must add that the incident kept me especially alert for some of those other emerging critters. The likes of bears and mountain lions would be looking to fatten up. Females would be birthing litters, calving, or laying eggs, or whatever. Spring ushered in a season of new life and new opportunity for man and beast.

As I'd learned with the cases I'd pursued during my time with the Texas Rangers, trains had become a speedy and reasonably efficient mode for traveling any significant distance. A two-week horseback ride from the ranch to Corsicana made no sense when a train could get me there in two days.

Thus, I left Tornado at home and rode one of our range horses to Corpus Christi. I stabled the cayuse there and took the train north to Corsicana. The only delays were a couple of train transfers that meant waiting patiently at depots.

It was a smooth, relaxing journey. For a change, I wasn't worried about being followed by some ne'er-do-well. The railroads were striving to improve the passenger experience. Padded seats sure were better than the wood slats of the past. The depots were another matter, as seating and grub could be quite inconsistent.

Corsicana had become wild and woolly. When I'd last visited, the oil field had been a sprawling work in progress. With the Spindletop gusher, all hell had broken loose. In the manner of iron filings to a magnet, men had come in droves to seek fame and fortune drilling for Texas crude. The black gold of Texas had supplanted the yellow gold of the Rockies. Deadwood and Sutter's Mill simply couldn't compare.

Archer Parr had given me the names of a couple of folks to look up toward hiring a drilling crew. Parr had pulled a string or two with Governor Culberson and John Reagan to sort of lubricate my introductions. My success in bringing down the Irish Mob also served to be a positive factor. The men running the rigs would hold my accomplishment in good stead. That wasn't to say it would be easy. These were tough people in a tough business. The men on the rigs faced danger every day. In fact, hardly a day went by that someone wasn't killed or seriously injured. I reminded myself that safety standards were absent. Common sense ruled, and there wasn't much of that.

Despite the edge that Parr and my own limited experience gave me, I knew that this would not be easy.

# NINETEEN
# FRUSTRATIONS

CORSICANA ITSELF HAD BOOMED in my absence. There seemed to be a saloon just about everywhere I looked. The station master who welcomed me told me that there were three dozen saloons and at least eight hotels and inns now gracing the neighborhoods of the town. He suggested a couple of hotels, but I already knew where I reckoned to stay. My taste in hotels had been elevated since my experience at the Hotel Alexander in Corpus Christi and that fully first-class Denver Hotel in Victoria. I expect I had become spoiled.

As I looked up and down the main street, I saw rough-looking oil field laborers pass fashionably well-dressed ladies and gentlemen on its streets. It was easy to spot those who'd already achieved some success. It was as though I was looking at a sort of cross section of America. As if to complete the picture of Corsicana, the aroma of oil carried on the breezes from the oil fields and accumulated in the clothes of the city's residents. Oil had surely put Corsicana on the map.

I checked in at the Beaton Hotel on North Main Street

and figured to get a couple of good meals and solid bed rest before heading for the oil fields the next day. The hotel staff was friendly but stressed. The oil boom brought plenty of fine folks seeking opportunity, but the seedier side was also represented. There were men—and women—who came like scavengers to prey on the human carrion discarded by the boom. There were plenty of downtrodden oil magnate wannabees who sought relief from success or failure. Investment fraud, murder, rape, prostitution, robbery, and more littered the streets of Corsicana and bled into Navarro County all the way to the oil fields.

I'd done a bit of homework before heading north. McTiernan sent a message ahead of me to Navarro County Sheriff Wiley Robinson, Sr., alerting him as to my arrival. From what I'd learned, Robinson was reasonably reliable and on the law-abiding side of the badge. There seemed to often be a seedy side to lawmen of the west. I also learned that the Corsicana oil boom had qualified it to have its very own city marshal, L.W. Cole. I surmised that the impetus for a city marshal had been driven by an event shortly before my arrival in which a mob burned some fellow named Henderson at the stake. It appeared that vigilante justice was alive and well in Texas.

I wondered what my old acquaintance Deputy US Marshal Bass Reeves up in Oklahoma might have thought of that. Reeves was a morally sound lawman. He'd likely have bristled at anything resembling vigilante justice. I promised myself that I'd go and have a long chat with Reeves.

After considering renting a horse to ride out to the oil fields, I decided that I should look the part of a future Texas oil magnet or some version thereof, at least to the extent of hiring a carriage and driver. I even brought along a suit for the occasion. Admittedly, my trusty Smith & Wesson was lodged in a shoulder holster hidden beneath my coat. Notably, stepping out from the hotel after breakfast to a waiting carriage was a treat for this South Texas cowboy.

Off we went to the oil fields. Admittedly, it felt good to ride in style.

The oil fields had changed with the beginning of the oil boom. There were twice as many derricks since I'd last visited. The place was abuzz with action. Tankers came, filled with oil, and lumbered out. I sought one of the contacts Parr had given me. When he wished me luck, I had no inkling as to how much I'd need it.

Soon enough, we pulled up in front of a building labeled J.S. Cullinan Company. This outfit was one of the early developers of the Corsicana oil fields and stood out by virtue of having its own refinery. As I stepped from the carriage, I barely missed plunging my boot into a puddle of oily water. I scanned the area and strode up to the entrance. Donald Stoker was the name of the manager emblazoned on a plaque on the door. I was about to have my first encounter in the Texas oil business.

"Come in." A voice inside responded to my knock on the door.

I gave the door a push and stepped inside. "Howdy, I'm Lucas Dunn. Archie Parr said you might be of some assistance to me."

The man at the desk sighed resignedly. "Name's Don Stoker. I'd offer a smoke, but it has a kick." He laughed at his little joke. Fire was unwelcome around oil fields. He looked me up and down. "Well, you don't look like any roughneck or mud man. What can I do for you, Mr. Dunn?"

"I've had some past connection with the oil business in

Texas, Mr. Stoker. Actually visited Corsicana a couple of times last year on business of sorts. To be straight with you, I own a ranch near Corpus Christi, and I believe there's oil on the property. I've acquired equipment and supplies but am now looking to hire a drilling crew."

I might as well have hit him up the side of his head with a branding iron. "Good crews are hard to come by, Mr. Dunn. You see plenty of men around here, but most aren't worth the boots they're walking in. If you're looking for me to help you find you a crew, you've come to the wrong place. I have good, hard-working crews and am pressed to find acceptable replacements when I lose any of them. You can check Lone Star, Navarro, or most any other company here, and you'll get the same answer. Sorry."

I appreciated that Stoker was being straight with me. I realized that, with the Spindletop gusher, the oil fields would quickly be overrun with roughneck wannabees. Any men I might find that were not employed by an existing company were likely to be unworthy of my consideration. "Well, I appreciate your time and advice, Mr. Stoker. Have a nice day." I turned to exit.

"One piece of advice before you go, Mr. Dunn. The venture you're describing on your ranch sounds as risky as they come. Plus, you're a small operation located far from the oil fields around here. I'll grant you that you might find oil, but you're going to be hard-pressed to get it refined without a refinery close by. There are folks out there who'd think nothing of stealing a tanker full of Texas crude, so transporting a long distance is a nonstarter. I'd be right careful were I in your boots."

"Thanks kindly," I said and stepped outside into the oil-laden air.

"Sir?" called my driver.

"Back to the Beaton Hotel," I told the driver and took

my seat in the carriage. I wasn't about to give up on my dream, but Stoker made great sense. An idea struck me, and I decided to have a conversation with Sheriff Robinson. I sucked in a whiff of the Texas crude in the air, and we headed to the hotel.

★★

I found myself sitting in a chair facing Sheriff Robinson's desk while he rooted through some papers. His office might have been typical of an old west lawman's office, except the oil boom had quite obviously increased the sheriff's workload. Three of the four cells held men apparently sleeping off the effects of too much booze. Two stacks of papers overloaded the trays on his desk, one teetering a tad and threatening to fall to the floor.

He finally set the papers on the desk and gave me what could best be described as a jaundiced once-over. He leaned forward, nearly knocking over one of the paper stacks. "So, you're from down Corpus way. McTiernan mentioned you." He took a long pull on a fat cigar stuck beneath a healthy growth of mustache. "You were a Texas Ranger, as I hear tell. You own a big spread near Nuecestown."

"Yes, sir. You've heard right," I stated. It appeared that McTiernan had shared just enough to establish my *bona fides*.

"So, what brings you to Corsicana?" he asked.

"The oil business. Mine."

"What has that to do with me?" queried Robinson. He raised an eyebrow questioningly.

"Well, I'm hoping we might help each other. I reckon you run into all sorts of characters in a town crawling with folks in the oil business, wanting to be in it, or taking advantage of it. I'm looking for a foreman to put a crew together to bring in a well I figure to drill in South Texas."

"And?" Robinson grunted. Now both eyebrows were raised with apprehension.

"I figure that you must have your ear to the rails around this town, Sheriff." I figured to appeal to the man's ego. "There might be a man out there mired in the competitive intensity of the Corsicana oil fields who's unhappy with his condition in life—at least as concerns the oil business. It sure would be a blessing to have such a person sent my way. I can offer far less intense conditions."

Robinson gave me a *what's in it for me* look.

Bribery was a fact of life in many western towns, and boom towns were especially rife with it. A few well-placed dollars could accomplish a lot. I sighed. "I can make it worth your while, *Sheriff*." I put a bit of emphasis on his title to let him know that I wasn't exactly pleased with the under-the-table rewarding of favors. I felt as though it sullied whatever good name remained of the lawman profession.

"You planning to be in town for a few days, Mr. Dunn?" asked Robinson.

"I'm staying at the Beaton," I said with finality.

"I'll see what I can do." With that, Robinson knocked the ashes off his cigar, gave a wry smile, and went back to shuffling papers.

I felt a little dirty walking back to the hotel, and it wasn't from the oil hanging in the air.

I walked relaxed-like past the front desk the next morning to go and enjoy some breakfast.

"Mr. Dunn? I've got a message for you," called the desk clerk. He rushed over to me with a slip of paper in hand.

"Thanks kindly," I said, taking the note. I then realized the young man was still standing before me with an anticipatory expression on his face. Did everything warrant reward? I gave him a *you've got to be kidding* sort of look. He looked a tad hangdog and went on his way. With that, I took a gander at the message. It was from Sheriff Robinson, advising me that he'd found someone who might interest me. I decided the matter could rest until after breakfast. I never cared to conduct business on an empty stomach.

I did enjoy a delicious meal before heading over to see Robinson. I knocked on his door but didn't wait for an invitation. It turned out that I awakened the sheriff from a nap.

"Oh…Dunn," he said groggily.

"You sent me a message?" I asked by way of reminding him.

"Max Johnson," he said.

I shrugged. "Who?" I kept my voice low so as to respect his condition.

Robinson squinted at me. "Back yonder. Cell number three." He managed to point in the direction of a row of iron-barred cells.

I nodded. "What about it?"

"Found a foreman for you." The sheriff sighed, as though it hurt to think or talk. "He just got fired from Lone Star and put on a drunk. He cold-cocked three roughnecks in a saloon. I jailed him until he sobers up." Robinson forced a smile.

I reckoned that the sheriff might have been sleeping off some of his own overindulging. He looked as though he'd fall back asleep at any second, so I turned and headed to the cells. Johnson couldn't be missed. He was a big man snoring like a locomotive. "Johnson?" I said in a normal tone so as not to disturb Robinson any further. Johnson didn't budge. I thought about calling his name louder, but decided to let him awaken on his own. I had time, and Johnson was going nowhere. I grabbed the chair from next to the sheriff's desk and sat back to wait.

I'd guess that I sat there for another half hour. I studied Johnson's inert form. He was obviously a man of some strength. Would he be savvy enough to run my rig? What had gotten him fired? I heard a groan from Johnson's direction. "Johnson?" I whispered.

"Dear God, what hit me?" moaned Johnson.

I'd never been drunk, so I could only guess from past observations that Johnson's head likely felt as though it was ten sizes too big and hurt like holy hell.

Johnson didn't raise his head. He opened one red-rimmed eye and looked at me. Suddenly, he leaned over the edge of the bed and barfed his guts out. There was an extended groan as he collapsed back on the bed. Using a massive forearm, he wiped what remained of the vomit from around his mouth. It was a struggle, but he finally raised his head enough to take another look at me. "Who the hell are you?" He looked around, and before I could answer, he blurted, "Where the hell am I?"

"I'm Luke Dunn, and you're in jail," I said evenly.

Johnson managed to sit up. "Dunn?" he asked.

I nodded. "Sheriff said you got in a bit of trouble last night."

"Not John Dunn?" he seemed concerned about the Dunn name.

"No, I'm Luke Dunn. But I have plenty of cousins named John. That a problem?" I responded.

By now, Johnson had managed to sit on the edge of the bed. He nearly put a foot in his vomit. "Just so you ain't no

John Dunn," he stated. He gave me a more studied look, then scanned the cell. "Where the hell is the sheriff?"

"Sleeping," I replied.

"What do you want?"

"I'll get to that. How'd you manage to get fired from Lone Star?"

"Damned boss's son got sassy, and I clocked him a good one right across his chops. Put the sonofabitch out cold. The boss took none too kindly to that."

I reckoned that was about as honest an answer as I was going to get. I could only imagine what a punch from this massive hulk might feel like. I sure didn't want to ever experience it. I was a big man, but Johnson was at least fifty pounds heavier. "Thirsty?" I asked.

Johnson gave a slight nod.

I fetched a cup of whatever dark swill Robinson had in the coffee pot and gave it through the bars to Johnson.

Johnson took a swig. "Damn!" he said with a wince of pain and threw the cup across the cell. He looked me over head to toe. "What was it you wanted?"

"I'm fixing to drill an exploratory oil well down near Corpus Christi. I'm looking to pull together a crew."

"What's that got to do with me?" he queried. He was beginning to regain his senses.

"I know enough about the oil business to be dangerous. I need a man who can be my foreman. If you've been fired, I reckoned you might be looking for a job."

"Exploratory well? South Texas? Are you crazy?"

"Let's get some things straight, Johnson. I own a large ranch that includes a parcel of tar bog that holds promise of oil. I also earned a reputation as a kickass Texas Ranger who has brought a few folks to justice, both alive and dead. I have the land and the equipment. I need a crew."

"Can you get me out of here?" he asked.

I knew that Robinson would release him as soon as he was sober, but I played along. "I can get you out of here. Are you interested in what I proposed?" I guess it could be said that I was a bit desperate. "Can you pull together a crew and supervise my rig?"

"You say you have the equipment and supplies? Where's the nearest saloon?"

That wasn't the best question to ask me. "Nuecestown will be off limits until we have a gusher or dry hole."

"Understood." Johnson stood shakily. He was a couple of inches shorter than me, but I still wouldn't mess with him. He seemed to be the sort to have beside you in a fight. "I'll do it," he stated firmly. I reached through the bars, and we shook hands. In the ranching community, a handshake was a man's bond.

I turned to see Sheriff Robinson approaching with the ring of cell keys. "How are things working out?" he asked. Whatever had him napping earlier had passed, as he seemed to be a new man. "There is the matter of Mr. Johnson's fine for disorderly conduct."

Now, I understood what was in this for the sheriff. "And?" I pressed.

"Fifty dollars," he replied.

That was likely a month's wages for Robinson. I took a long, hard look at Johnson. "Okay, I'll hire him and bail him out." I dug deep and forked over fifty dollars.

# TWENTY
# THE CREW

A FULLY SOBER Max Johnson appeared to be capable. He seemed to have the respect of many of the laborers at the Corsicana oil fields. I overheard a couple of roughnecks talking about how the boss's son at Lone Star needed a whipping. They admired Johnson for not tolerating the young man's constant leveraging of his father's name to advantage. As some might say, beggars can't be choosy.

I told Johnson that I needed the full crew assembled in four days. We'd catch the train to Corpus Christi and then travel by wagon to the drill site. If all went well and the weather cooperated, I reckoned that we'd be drilling for black gold by the third week of April.

Johnson's challenge was to recruit men who were both capable and willing to leave what was steady work. The best I could do was pay top dollar. It increased my financial risk, but I insisted on capable labor. I had a bunkhouse of sorts with cooking facilities built near the drill site, along with a shed that would serve as a small but serviceable field office. I even had a road graded from the site to facilitate the movement of the tankers once we struck oil.

Bless Cassie's heart, she didn't raise an eyebrow or otherwise protest, as my project ate into our deposit at the Corpus Christi National Bank. She'd even learned that the vast majority of exploratory wells turned out dry. I'd heard a number like ninety percent. She never complained.

By the end of the first week in April, my crew of drillers, derrickmen, roughnecks, tool pushers, and mechanics was aboard a train headed south with me. It was a decidedly rough crew. Most looked as though oil was a second skin despite repeated bathings. As a whole, they seemed good-spirited. To a man, they were glad to have escaped the Corsicana grime, prostitution, drunken brawls, robberies, and murders.

Upon arrival in Corpus Christi, I bought a dinner for the men and boarded them at a local inn rather than push through to the ranch at night. A few rain showers were passing, so it would have been a miserable introduction to South Texas.

Johnson assembled the crew at dawn and got them piled into the wagon. I freed my gelding from the stable and led the way to the drill site. I decided to not take the crew past my house and the ranch operations buildings. They weren't cowboys, and there was no point in introducing them to that side of my business.

We arrived at the drill site around midday. Johnson immediately went to work examining the supplies and equipment I'd gathered together. "You seem to have thought of everything, Mr. Dunn," he said loudly enough for the crew to hear. He wanted the men holding me in utmost respect. I was the source of their pay after all. If this exploratory well hit paydirt, they were well aware that there'd be more work.

I stood facing the crew. They wore pretty much what they left Corsicana with. They looked at me expectantly and respectfully. I sure was a contrast appearance-wise. There I was wearing ranch garb from cowboy hat to polished boots. My pants were even held up by a newfangled thing called a belt. "Welcome to The Heaven's Gate Oil Company. The next few weeks will be a test of the promise of oil in South Texas. You'll work hard. I know it's dangerous, so I can only urge you to be careful." I knew that most deadly incidents were beyond the control of the crews. An errant spark could cause a fire, explosion, or both. "I have duties back at ranch headquarters, so I ask you to do as Mr. Johnson here directs. When—not if—the well comes in, there will be bonuses. It will have been worth your hard work." With that, I left the crew to settle in the bunkhouse while Johnson and I headed for the field office.

"We'll get underway with site preparation this afternoon, Mr. Dunn. We'll need solid footings for that derrick over yonder," Johnson said with a nod toward the rig lying nearby.

"I don't figure to meddle, Max. I hired you to run the drilling operations. If all goes well, you'll do well." I shook his hand. "My cowhands may stop by to watch out of idle curiosity. I'll try not to have them be a distraction."

"One final question before you go," said Johnson with a thoughtful pose. "Is yours the only exploratory well around here?"

"So far as I know, it is. There may yet be others, but I know of no other tar bogs like we have here. I do think we have a great chance of success."

Johnson smiled. "Is ranching and law enforcement profitable?"

It was a strange question for an oilman to ask. I smiled. "Ranching can be so long as there are no droughts. Being a lawman? Decidedly unprofitable. Oil entails great risk but far greater profitability." I found it notable that Johnson had shed his more colloquial language.

"I'd say putting your life on the line as a lawman is the riskiest." He grinned. "To be honest, I did a bit of homework about you, Mr. Dunn. I admire your accomplishments. I look forward to bringing this well in."

With that, I left for home. I didn't want to be seen as hovering over my foreman.

The meeting with the crew had tired me more than I'd expected. I guess it was more emotionally draining than I cared to admit. I mulled this over as I sat with Cassie at our kitchen table. Sean and Bode played in a corner while baby Carolyn napped.

"Did you see the *Caller-Times* this morning?" Cassie asked as she sipped her coffee.

I shook my head.

She pushed the newspaper toward me. She had folded it to display an article that had caught her eye. "Remember Chato?" Her eyes spoke concern.

How could we ever forget Chato and his savage attack upon us? I put my coffee aside and took a gander at the article Cassie had brought to my attention. The headline brought attention to ongoing Apache problems along the Rio Grande toward Laredo. I recalled how my dad had dealt with bandits around there and, of course, some Apache.

The piece in the newspaper went on to describe predations being led by Chato's remaining son, Tochin. Apparently, the proverbial fruit didn't fall far from the tree. No doubt, the death of his father and brother at our hands put us at risk of the young warrior's wrath. I knew enough Apache to know that Tochin's name translated to Mountain Lion. I reflexively glanced at the mountain lion skin decorating our parlor wall. "Seems to always be something to be concerned about. Will this thing called civilization ever conquer the evils of men?" In a sense, it was a rhetorical question.

"They haven't caught him, Lucas," she replied. "Civilization or not, these savages must be stopped."

Her sentiments rang true. The price of these rogue Apache and other tribes preying on ranches and towns along the border needed to end. I was sure that Captain Hughes had his hands full. We were long beyond debating whether conquering tribal lands was a moral or not. It seemed to be a cultural imperative. I sighed resignedly. "Seems it isn't showing signs of ceasing. Better keep the Winchester handy." The mention of the carbine tossed a harsh dose of reality upon us.

"You better watch your back trail, Lucas Dunn," she cautioned.

She was like my mom—maybe like many wives—using my full name to drive home a concern. "I'll be careful. We'll do our range riding in pairs again."

"I'll keep the dogs close, too. They aren't fighters, but they do make for an early warning of intruders."

I smiled. Brody and Tess hadn't been much help against that Apache attack. They were sweet dogs and good hunters, but not guard dogs.

## TWENTY-ONE
# TROUBLE THIS WAY COMES

I CHECKED on work progress every couple of days. I sure as shootin' didn't want to get in Johnson's way. The men seemed to respond well to his direction, and there was no point in messing with that. By the first week of May, the derrick was up and drilling had commenced.

Johnson had chosen what he figured to be the most promising spot to drill.

"Feeling confident in the spot you chose, Max?" I asked, as we sat in the field office.

Johnson shrugged. "Seemed good as any, boss."

"We should know something in a couple of weeks," I said by way of a wild prediction.

"We're drilling at a goodly pace, Mr. Dunn. Doing about seventy-five feet or so per day. The soil is soft, so sinking casings has slowed us a bit."

"Any problems?"

"Couple of the men got a little mouthy, but I handled that. The men get restless." Johnson gave a twist to his mustache. "They likely need a day or two off."

"You've been drilling for five days now. Another five,

and we'll reach the same depth as Spindletop. You'll want the men fresh when that rig gushes oil." I was optimistic to say the least. "I guess a day or two off will do them good."

"The crew will be pleased. I didn't want to give them time off without checking with you. It'll be good for morale."

I was impressed that he'd asked. Johnson was apparently concerned that, if he gave the men time off, I might think they weren't working hard enough and be upset with his supervision. "How much further do you think we must drill?" I asked.

"As far as we must drill, boss." By now, Johnson was understanding that I had a sense of humor.

I was prepared for a vague answer and appreciated Johnson's veiled optimism. Drilling for oil was rough, dangerous work. It was no place for the weak of mind or body.

The sun crested the eastern horizon on a spectacular May morning.

"Do you think we're getting close?" asked Cassie, as she whipped up breakfast.

I sat sipping my coffee and reading the newspaper. "Johnson says we're about halfway the depth at which they found oil at Spindletop. Likely be another couple of weeks. The soft soil slows the process a bit owing to inserting casings to support the shaft."

"You're becoming quite the oilman, Lucas," she replied admiringly.

"Max seems to be working out. We've given the crew a couple of days off, so they'll be fresh for what we hope will be the final big push."

"Are they going to Nuecestown?" she asked.

"I reckon," I said with a smile. "They're rough men. I hope they're gentle with the town."

"Maybe, you should let Sheriff McTiernan know."

"Hopefully, there'll be no trouble, but you're probably right. I'll give him a call." I began to dig into the heaping pile of eggs and bacon Cassie had set before me. An item in the newspaper caught my eye. "Looks like more trouble at the border. That Mexican president sure has his hands full." My eyes fell to a short article beneath the news from the border. "Lookee here. They're giving me credit for solving the murder of cousin Nick's ranch hand and the killing of cattle around the region. Funny, they never mention that the killer was a vegetarian and how it fed his motives."

Cassie raised an eyebrow and smiled. "Heaven forbid they should offend anyone who doesn't eat steaks, Lucas," she said sarcastically and gave a little laugh. "I'm sure Mr. Kleberg is happy," she said, then added, "I'll bet Captain Hughes is chaffing at his bit with wishing you were helping on the Rio Grande."

I laughed. "He can keep right on chaffing at the bit."

"You lily-livered, horse-whipped sonofabitch! Who you callin' a coward?" hollered the drunken roughneck.

Four cowboys, far more sober than the oil laborers, found themselves facing the four fully inebriated roughnecks. "Don't be bitin' off more than y'all can chew, fellas," advised one of the cowboys. He was the biggest of the four ranch hands who'd come to Nuecestown for a bit of food, fun, and beer. Cody Wahls was his name, and there weren't but two or three men in all of South Texas who stood a chance against him in a fight.

One roughneck hurled a beer stein at the cowboys just as Sheriff McTiernan walked through the batwing doors. It sailed over the cowboys' heads and narrowly missed the sheriff, as it smashed to pieces against the doorjamb.

"You boys are deputized," said McTiernan to the cowboys. "Let's get these troublemakers to jail."

With that, the roughnecks charged headlong at the cowboys. Sober, they might have stood a chance. A few hard punches were thrown. Fists and heads were bloodied. A chair was broken over a roughneck's head. In the space of five minutes, McTiernan was leading a contingent of cowboys hauling roughnecks to the tiny Nuecestown jail.

"Thanks kindly, boys," said a grateful sheriff with a satisfied grin. "These outsiders should know better than to mess with South Texas cowpokes."

The cell housed four roughnecks nursing hangovers and bruises to bodies and egos. They were gradually waking up as Sheriff McTiernan eased his way from the battered old desk with the key ring in hand. He'd managed to grab some shuteye and even heated up some of the dark swill that passed for jail coffee.

McTiernan took a long look at the four red-eyed, sorry excuses for manhood that sat about the cell. A couple of them had peed in their pants and stunk to high heaven. "You men find your way back to Dunn's oil well. Next time you figure to tear up Nuecestown, you can count on serious jail time," McTiernan was warning the four roughnecks locked in the cells of the Nuecestown jail. He appreciated that Junior had given him a heads-up. Had he not been in town, the men might have caused serious damage. He turned as a man entered.

Johnson stood at the doorway with a shotgun cradled on his arm. "Howdy, I'm Max Johnson. These men cause trouble?" Of course, he knew they had. Roughnecks were a hard-living lot, and last night they'd hard-lived up to that characterization.

"You're working for Lucas Dunn, aren't you?" asked McTiernan.

"Yes, sir," responded Johnson.

McTiernan sighed. "Well, next time, I'll be fining y'all." The sheriff proceeded to free the men from the cells. He grabbed the elbow of the last man out and turned toward the sheriff. "Keep an eye on this one, Mr. Johnson. He was the worst of them last night."

The roughneck appeared as though he wanted to curse the sheriff but decided to not press his luck.

"We've got drilling yet to do, Sheriff. We'll try to stay out of trouble." Johnson glared at the four roughnecks and led them away.

Once out of earshot of the jail, Johnson stopped them. "I told you men to stay out of trouble. Do this sort of thing again, and I'll send you all back to Corsicana with nothing but the shirts on your backs—after I've whipped your sorry asses. Do I make myself understood?"

There were grudging nods all around.

"Yer a big man with thet scattergun, boss man," said Bill Squires, the roughest of the group.

"Don't test me, Squires," warned Johnson. "Now, get your asses back to the drill site."

Squires sneered menacingly but held his tongue, as they piled into the wagon Johnson had driven to town in anticipation of what he'd be finding.

☆☆

I arrived at the drill site around mid-morning with Jake beside me, just as Johnson and four of his crew pulled in. The rest of the crew were mostly at work. They anxiously awaited the other men, as some job functions needed more manpower. Looking at the four, it wasn't difficult to figure out what had happened. Johnson flashed me a *don't ask* look as he shook his head disdainfully. He had some trouble-makers, and he was none too happy about it.

"Looks like their rest in Nuecestown wasn't so restful, boss," Jake whispered, so the roughnecks couldn't overhear him.

"Rough men rest rough, I guess," I responded with a chuckle. "You, Pedro, and Jimmy have been known to tie on a good one at the saloon. Don't be the pot calling the kettle black," I chided.

"You think the well will come in?" asked Jake.

"Yes. Yes, I do," I replied. I nodded at Johnson, signaling that I had no problem with however he'd handled his crew. "Let's go check for strays," I said to Jake.

We turned and headed away from the drill site.

"You expect anything to change if that well comes in?" asked Jake.

I sensed a bit of worry embedded in the question. "You'll get a better saddle," I joked.

"Pedro, Jimmy, and I have been wondering, boss." Jake was concerned, and I'd just brushed him off.

I pulled up and looked off thoughtfully into the distance. "I understand, Jake. I expect there'll be more money to support ranch operations. We'll pay you better. But I really hadn't given thought to any big changes in life-style. The Dunn family in Texas has never hobnobbed with the monied folks, so I suspect nothing will change all that much."

Jake smiled. "We suspected not."

We spurred our horses and headed out. We hadn't ridden but a couple of hundred yards, and an explosion from the drill site tore the air.

"That's a shotgun," I observed. "A big one!" I turned Tornado back toward the drill site.

We reined in to find Johnson staring down three roughnecks. A crater had been blown in the ground about ten feet in front of the three men. "You men are finished. Get your damned asses out of here!" I overheard Johnson command them. "The next shot will be in your bellies."

How Johnson's shotgun was going to hit three men simultaneously was beyond the point. Somebody would be killed if they didn't leave.

The three gathered their gear and grudgingly began walking off.

"Weston!" called Johnson. "Get back here."

The man named Weston paused as the other two continued to walk away.

"You're worth a second chance. You can stay, if you'll behave."

Weston looked at the two who were leaving and then at Johnson as though trying to decide between income and loyalty to a couple of ne'er-do-wells. "I'll behave, Mr. Johnson," he finally said and walked back to the camp.

"Nicely done," I said by way of compliment to Johnson.

Johnson shrugged. "Now, we're short two men. It'll slow us a little, Mr. Dunn, but we'll get it done." He turned and shouted to one of the men. "Careful with that casing, damn it!"

"I'll leave you be," I said and rode off with Jake. We headed back to the fence line.

"They're rough," he observed.

"Seems like most anything worth doing takes effort, Jake. Look at the hard work we put in at branding time or those long dusty days driving cattle to the railheads. But we're free, Jake. We are free to choose what we want to do with our lives. Hard work, yes. Satisfying, you bet." I was feeling philosophical. A lesser man than Jake might have rolled their eyes. "By what I've seen and my dad taught, folks generally don't lose their freedom by the might of others, they usually lose it because they let someone else define it. They're too lazy to make their own choices and surrender to the convenience provided by others. From the very beginnings of mankind, men have tried to exercise dominion over other men."

Jake was listening attentively.

"There was a time, Jake, when folks coming west would find a piece of land in the vastness of the mountains and prairies and simply claim it. Now, the government chooses what we can and can't claim. Freedom has been lost."

"Takes a strong man to buck against the folks that steal our freedoms, boss," observed Jake.

"Wealth and power, Jake. Without the wealth that gives you power, the powerful—be they politicians, businessmen, lawbreakers, or just rich folks with an axe to grind—will chew you up and spit you out."

"I hope that well comes in, boss," said Jake earnestly. He had begun to understand how the riches from oil would provide a shield against loss of freedoms.

We spent the rest of the day rounding up stray beeves and even a couple of horses. The weather was taking a turn from mild to searingly hot, as made less tolerable by humidity. Texas weather was not the place for the faint of heart.

Oil…crude…black gold…Texas tea…it's all the same black liquid spawned from the depths of the land. Grass sure wasn't growing under my feet. In my mere twenty-eight years, I'd been a lawman bringing outlaws to justice, a rancher raising cattle, a fighter fending off Comanche and Apache, and now an oilman looking to bring in my first well. Above all, I was a husband and parent. The casual observer might say that I led a full life. Well, there'd be no argument from me. Mind you, I'm not a prideful man, but I sure do take pride in everything I do.

The drilling operation had been going on for about three weeks. The trouble we had with a couple of the roughnecks and the consequent short-staffed crew slowed us down just a little. I had to hand it to Johnson, as he seemed able to pull maximum effort from his charges.

"Reckon to head to the drill site, sweetheart," I mumbled through a mouthful of eggs and venison sausage. "Johnson says that we're a tad deeper than a thousand feet. That's near the depth that the Lucas gusher up at Spindletop came in."

"You think it's about due?" asked Cassie. There was no hiding her anxiety.

"Any day," I replied optimistically. I was already beyond anxiety. While I knew that a dry well wouldn't suck us dry financially, there was something in me that wanted South Texas to enter the oil boom. That well needed to bring oil; lots of it.

Cassie was about to sip her coffee, when she paused. She put the cup on the table and gave me the strangest, faraway sort of look, as though possessed by some sort of spirit. "Lucas, today is the day." She said it so convincingly that I couldn't doubt it for a second.

I sat silently for a moment. "Yes, you're right. I believe you're right."

I finished breakfast, tussled with the boys for a few minutes, kissed Cassie, and soon found myself riding southeastward toward our rig.

As I approached the rig, there seemed to be more activity than I'd noted from previous observations. I hitched Tornado near the office shack. I hollered to Johnson, but he paid me no mind. The crew was intently focused on the drill hole.

Finally, Johnson looked up and saw me. He raised both hands as though warning me to stand back.

I froze. Something was happening. Were I to hazard a guess, we were about to learn the fate of our oil well.

Suddenly, the men stepped away from the rig. There was some vibration. Now, the men dove for cover. Oil blew skyward. A huge column of crude spewed high from the drill head. I felt windblown droplets of oil against my face and looked down to see my clothes taking in the black gold mist. I fought the urge to back away to the shack.

The cheering crew was bathed in oil. Johnson raised a fist and delivered a huge grin at me.

Admittedly, I sported a smile that was at least a mile wide. I found myself drawn to the well; oil bath be praised.

The crew members were yelling, back-slapping, and shouting for joy.

And oil gushed to the heavens.

Now, I'd heard that it took about ten days to cap the gusher at Spindletop. Folks estimated that a hundred thousand barrels a day was lost before they had it under control.

Blessedly, Johnson had anticipated the gusher and had the equipment needed to cap it. The good news was that they would, in fact, be able to cap the well, the less-good news was that it would take a couple of days until the pressure subsided enough to enable the crew to cap it. Meanwhile, we'd be watching Texas crude spouting for all the world to see.

I looked around behind me to see the side of the shack dripping with oil. Thankfully, I'd hitched Tornado on the side of the building away from the drill site. My trusty stallion was spared an oil bath.

"Hallelujah! Hallelujah!" I hollered at Johnson. "Damn, Max! You brought her in!" I slapped an oily hand on his back.

"I knew it would come in, boss," he replied, still wearing his mile-wide grin.

The joy fest went on for a good hour.

I could hardly wait to tell Cassie and our ranch hands. As I dwelled on sharing the ecstatic happiness of the well coming in, it struck me that I might have created a monster. Just as the opportunists of every stripe had flocked to Beaumont and Corsicana, word would get out, and they'd be tumbling all over themselves to plant rigs around South Texas. I felt pressed to get my operation under control as quickly as possible. The oil had to be placed in tankers, transported to market, and sold. Equally important in my mind was more wells. Yep, I envisioned an oil field to rival Corsicana.

While the men continued to celebrate, Johnson and I walked to the office where we could talk without our voices being drowned out by gushing oil.

"You're going to need more men, Max," I said by way of opening the conversation.

He gave me a questioning look and then smiled. "More wells, boss?"

"You've earned your bonus. There'll be plenty more."

"You know men will flock here like moths to a flame," he said.

I frowned. "No flame, Max."

"Sorry, boss. Bad choice of words." He was still grinning.

"You up for the job ahead?" I pressed.

"The well had come in big, boss. I suspect there's no shortage of oil under us. But we'd better move quickly. Maybe add a couple more derricks out there." He paused thoughtfully. "Shame we couldn't have already had a couple of wells being drilled. It might have relieved the pressure on this one and made capping easier."

"I'm going to head home and give my family and the ranch hands the news. I know the men have been keeping an eye on y'all off and on, so they're looking forward to the good news."

"We'll get the well under control as soon as possible, boss. Don't you be worrying none."

With that, I wiped my face as best I could and headed out to share the news at home.

I reined in at the hitching rail in front of our house and literally slid from Tornado's saddle. Suffice to say, the leather was well-oiled. I glanced down at myself and realized that I was quite a sight to behold. I might have been mistaken for the gusher itself.

I had the good sense to not be dripping oil inside the house that Cassie so meticulously kept clean. So, I knocked.

There was no answer.

I knocked again and heard Cassie's footsteps. I stepped to one side, so she wouldn't see me right off.

The door swung open. She couldn't help but catch a

whiff of oil aroma. "What on earth is that…?" She finally saw me. "Lucas Dunn! Oh my! Look at you!"

I swept her into my oily self in a great hug. "It's a gusher, Cassie!"

She stepped back, totally amazed. She'd been right this morning.

"Dang, but look at you, woman. You're a mess." I'd managed to share my oil, and she wore it well. I embraced her again and gave her a long, oily kiss. "Your hunch was right."

Cassie looked at the two of us, smeared with oil, and laughed. "That was no hunch, Lucas. I felt it in my bones. I just knew that well would come in."

Sean appeared in the doorway and scanned us head to toe. He pinched his nose between thumb and forefinger and made a face. Little Bode toddled up behind and mimicked him.

"Get used to it, boys," I assured them with a broad smile. I turned to Cassie. "It'll take a few days to cap it, then I'll take everyone down there to see the goings on."

It took a bit to clean ourselves up. With two rambunctious toddlers around, it wasn't easy to take a private bath sufficient to clean the oil from our bodies. It took a lot of scrubbing, which we managed to enjoy.

Finally cleaned up, Cassie and I sat at the kitchen table sipping coffee while I explained the next steps. "We're going to put up two more drill rigs, sweetheart. The word's going to get out faster than a prairie fire with a tailwind. Boomers will descend on South Texas looking to squeeze riches from everything associated with oil."

"Makes sense. Though I don't feature looking at oil derricks everywhere we turn."

The image of Corsicana came to mind. It amounted to a harsh dose of reality. Eventually, someone would find oil in

South Texas. Why not us? "I doubt that it'll be a course of history that we'll be able to change, sweetheart." I took a sip of coffee. "We'll try to be good stewards of the land, but there'll be no accounting for others."

"Wasn't that long ago that the range was free, Lucas."

I sure knew of what she spoke. It wasn't but thirty years back that barbed wire began its march across the rangelands. There'd been a time when a man could ride for days on end without ever seeing a fence. Roads, railroads, and fences carved the land, as mankind sought to master it. "Heard any more of that Apache?"

"Tochin?" she asked.

I nodded.

"I overheard some ladies in Corpus saying that he was stealing Mexican cattle and selling them to Texas ranchers, then rustling Texas cattle and selling them to Mexicans."

It was a practice that Apache chiefs like Cochise, Mangas Coloradas, Victorio, and Lozen had practiced along the border, further to the west. Tochin was simply following a proven business model. Regrettably, many ranchers on both sides of the border lost their lives to this thievery. "I'll have to remind Jake to keep our ranch hands on alert."

"Do you think Tochin will come here?" Cassie was quite clearly worried.

To have to worry about these things as close to Corpus Christi as was deeply concerning. Too often, we were fending off threats to ranch life that should have been stopped years ago. Whether rattlers, bears, or Indians, there seemed to be threats that we must handle, but others—like the Apache—that we should never have to worry about. "We just don't know, sweetheart. I suppose that depends on how far his hatred carries him." Knowing that we were a mere ninety or so miles from the Rio Grande tended to give us who'd grown up around these parts a special understanding of these things. "What's for dinner?" I asked by way of changing the subject.

Cassie smiled. "Ribs," she stated flatly, then smiled provocatively. "And a special dessert."

That would be a great way to celebrate the Heaven's Gate Oil Company gusher.

# TWENTY-TWO
# FIRE

AS I HEADED out to the stable, I patted the Winchester hanging beside the front door out of the reach of our sons. I reckoned to ride out and see how Johnson was making out toward capping the well. True to my policy of not riding alone, I borrowed Jimmy.

"Have you ridden out to the well site yet, Jimmy?" I asked by way of a conversation starter.

He nodded. His face said that he held a secret. "They be puttin' up more of them derricks, boss."

That got me to thinking as to what his secret was. Johnson wouldn't be putting up derricks if the gusher hadn't been capped. "Sounds like progress," I observed.

"There be more crew down there, too," he added.

So, Johnson was preparing to drill the additional wells. It would mean that we'd draw even more barrels of Texas crude. We'd soon be needing more than tankers to transport our oil. I understood that former Texas governor Hogg and a fellow named Swayne had formed a syndicate that was going to ship oil via a pipeline to a refinery at Port Arthur. It began with a pumping station and oil storage tanks.

"Whatcha thinkin' on, boss," interrupted Jimmy.

"That we've got a lot more than drilling to be getting done. We're going to have to build a pipeline, Jimmy. But more than that, we need a refinery close by and a channel for tanker ships." I found myself thinking aloud on aspects that I hadn't given enough thought to, despite all my planning. I heard someone say, *"Man plans, God laughs."* That's because man never develops the perfect plan. As I thought on this oil discovery, I realized that we were going to have to do what Hogg and Swayne had done and form some sort of business arrangement to build the infrastructure to handle the great quantities of oil we'd be pumping from the ground. I gave a laugh. "Guess I'm thinking on a lot, Jimmy."

We rode the rest of the way mostly in silence. Admittedly, I was thinking on whom we might want to draw into a syndicate. We'd need a team with the resources to overcome any opposition to something as critically important as a pipeline crossing ranch or farmland. The specter of an oil leak in a field of cotton or ruining the grasses of pasture land would pose challenges to be overcome. Storage tanks and oil pumps would dot the land. They weren't exactly pieces of fine art to be admired. Cassie was right about being good stewards of the land, but pipelines—like the railroads—would become part of the lives of Texans.

While my mind was on the oil business, I began to get the feeling that we were being watched. Maybe, it was Cassie's concern with Tochin, the rogue Apache, working on my mind. Still, it was an eerie sort of sensation. I reflexively scanned around us. Naturally, I saw nothing concerning. No self-respecting Indian would want to be seen anyway.

★★

I couldn't miss the capped oil well as we approached the drill site. Johnson had managed to cap it in a mere five days. The bog around us was soaked with the thousands of barrels of oil that had gushed uncontrolled from the well. It was a loss that simply had to be absorbed; a cost of doing this business.

Johnson was at one of the far derricks, so I waved and motioned him to the office shack.

"What would yuh have me do, boss?" asked Jimmy.

There was no point in his listening in on my meeting with Johnson. I thought a second. "Take a ride around. See if you find any sign of folks who shouldn't be around here."

"Like Apache?" Jimmy responded.

I nodded. I appreciated that he was aware of the possible threat. "Like Apache," I repeated by way of reinforcement. I gazed out over the rolling grasslands. The sandy-loam soil didn't lend itself to tracking, but there might be other sign like horse droppings and even lost personal belongings. The Apache didn't wear feathered headdresses like many Comanche did, so feathers would be an unlikely find. Shiny objects were more the Apache style.

I watched Jimmy ride off as Johnson came in.

"Mornin', Mr. Dunn," greeted Johnson. "What can I do for you today?"

"Congratulations on getting the well capped and starting on the other two." I shook Johnson's hand, and we entered the office. "I have a couple of concerns that we need to discuss."

"Problems, boss?" he asked.

"Concerns. I've realized that we need to more efficiently transport oil. The folks up near Beaumont and Corsicana are building pipelines to a refinery at Port Arthur. I want to do the same thing here. Like them, I'll be working to put a syndicate together. It's going to require far more resources than I can draw on right now, and I refuse to take on debt."

"I figured that you'd head down that road, boss," responded Johnson thoughtfully. "We're building storage tanks and will have the pump operational tomorrow."

"Great. That was one of my other concerns."

"You have more?" he asked.

I could see that Johnson was anxious to return to supervising the new drilling rigs. "Yes," I answered.

Johnson grew serious as he sensed the concern on my face.

"Apache," I said.

"Those savages from way south of here?" he responded.

"Those savages attacked Heaven's Gate a couple of months back. We fought them off, but it was nasty. They've been raiding along the Rio Grande, but the warrior leading them is the son of the Apache leader we killed in the attack on our home. His name is Tochin. We've killed his father and brother and reckon he's holding on to some hate for us. Vengeance could be in play."

"What would you have us do?" Johnson naturally asked.

"I'm going to send a few rifles down here to keep here in the office and hire a man to keep a lookout and provide an early warning of any possible attack."

"You think they'd attack an oil field?"

"They likely don't even know what one is, Max. But, they might see it as despoiling the land; their land." I hoped that Johnson wouldn't be chased off by the prospect of an Indian raid.

"They still take scalps?" he chided. "We'll deal with them, boss. Don't you be worrying none."

"One last thing. I figure to bring the family by in a

couple of days. Don't be cleaning up for that. I want them to see how it is."

"No problem," he replied. "By the way, we do need more tankers, boss. Those additional wells are going to increase production."

"I'm on it. I'll see you in a couple of days."

I mounted Tornado and began keeping an eye out for Jimmy. I figured he couldn't have ranged very far in the few minutes I'd spent with Johnson. I made out what appeared to be his horse's hoofprints in the dry sandy soil. They headed toward a grassy knoll up ahead. I didn't especially cotton to the way I was feeling, so I eased Tornado along while scanning the horizon. I simply had a sense that danger lurked. Maybe I was being too sensitive.

I decided to ride around the knoll rather than over its top. It took a bit longer, but it made sense from a caution viewpoint. As I rounded the far end of the grassy knoll, I saw Jimmy's horse. The saddle was empty. I dismounted and walked toward the cayuse while holding Tornado's reins.

A motion several hills away caught my eye. It appeared to be a horseman galloping away. From what little I could make out of the clothing, it might have been an Apache. That caused me to be extra alert as I searched for my ranch hand.

I finally found Jimmy lying beside a cactus. He was unconscious. I saw no wounds, though he had a good-sized lump on the side of his head. I assumed that he came upon an Apache scout who clubbed him and got away fast. It was likely the person I'd seen riding off. As Jimmy struggled to come to, I made a quick survey of the surrounding area. There were horse tracks leading in the general direction of the figure I'd seen riding away.

I managed to get Jimmy to regain consciousness. Other than a nasty headache, he seemed okay. "What happened?" I naturally asked as I sought to confirm my suspicions.

"Don't know, boss. I dismounted to examine what I thought was a shiny concho. That's the last thing I remember."

If the attacker was an Apache, the hostiles were coming too close for comfort. "I think you might have been attacked by an Apache."

Jimmy felt for his hair.

"It's okay. He must have seen me coming and had no time to scalp you." I chuckled at my own humor, though the situation was serious. "You feel up to riding?"

Jimmy nodded gently.

"I've got to warn Johnson that hostiles are in the area, then we'll head back home." I knew that I must move quickly to get weapons to Johnson to defend themselves in the event that Tochin was of a mind to attack.

We warned Johnson and headed for home at a gallop. I expect that Jimmy's head throbbed with every stride of his horse, but he didn't complain. I had been determined to get weapons to the oil drilling site no later than the next morning, but now I felt compelled to do it this evening, even if it meant getting home after nightfall. If one Apache scout was lurking, a war party couldn't be far away.

I assembled Jake and the other hands at the barn. I'd already told Cassie what I was up to. We didn't tell Sean and Bode, as we didn't want to traumatize them. There was no way I was going to endure another surprise attack on our home. Any Apache would find Heaven's Gate Ranch armed and ready. To that end, I set up a round-the-clock watch. Each of the ranch hands was to carry a rifle and sidearm at all times, even to the outhouse.

Through it all, I wondered where the Texas Rangers or even the Army were. They must have known what was going on. Was the young buck warrior Tochin so stealthy that he could sneak around South Texas undetected? The word *ineptitude* crept across my thinking. Mind you, I wasn't totally blaming them, they just didn't seem to be in the right places when needed.

I pulled together five rifles that I'd found at my dad's house: three Winchesters, a Henry, and a Spencer. They would have to do for now. I loaded them on a packhorse along with what I reckoned to be plenty enough ammunition and headed for the drill site.

It was late afternoon when I reined in at the drill site office and entered.

Johnson had seen me coming and met me inside the office. "Been quiet, boss. I think you might be overreacting."

What did Johnson know about fighting Indians, especially hostile Apache? The damned savages could steal a man's mustache without him knowing it. "It's when you don't think they're around that they're suddenly in your face, Max. I saw that scout earlier today, and Jimmy has a lump on his head to prove their intentions."

Johnson sighed. "As you say." He still wasn't convinced.

I found myself curious as to why, if they were planning to attack, they hadn't stopped me from bringing weapons to the drill site. As I considered this, yelling erupted from the direction of the wells. Gunfire filled the air.

Johnson and I grabbed rifles and headed to the window.

Roughnecks were diving for cover, and at least two had been struck by Apache bullets.

"There's my overreaction, Max," I hollered and smashed out the windowpane. I began pouring lead at the attacking Apache.

Johnson gave it his all, but he wasn't the skilled shooter that I was. He fumbled with the lever action, and I had to reload the carbine for him. Time was wasting, and our crew was outnumbered.

To my horror, I saw three Apache approach the well head. It was happening in a sort of slow motion right before my eyes. They opened the valve just a little and struck a match.

The explosion must have been heard all the way to Corpus Christi. The three savages were killed instantly, plus a handful of Apache and roughnecks nearby. The remaining window in the shed was shattered.

The Apache retreated, and Johnson and I looked out into the searing heat of a column of fire.

"Damn, Max! How do we put out the fire?" I hollered over the conflagration.

Johnson looked at a stack of boxes sitting undisturbed in a corner of the shed.

The boxes were labeled *DYNAMITE*. What the hell they were doing stored in the office was beyond me, but Johnson seemed to think we'd need them. "How much?" I asked.

"All of it," replied Johnson.

"How does it work?" I pressed him, as I felt the heat from the fire radiate through the shack. At this point, I was praying that the heat didn't set off the explosives.

"Explosion creates a shock wave that starves the fire of oxygen," he advised. "No oxygen, no fire."

"How do we get it there?" It was my next logical question.

Johnson showed total fear for the first time. He gave a *not-me* shrug.

So, getting the dynamite to the well head was going to be my job. "Do you have anything to put it in?" It seemed obvious that the wooden boxes the dynamite was stored in weren't up to the task.

"There's a steel drum behind the shack," he told me.

I glared at Johnson. Was he figuring to do nothing? "Damn!" I exclaimed. I was resigned to my fate. Somebody had to do this, and it looked as though it would be me. "I'll go around back. Hand the dynamite to me through the window." I dashed behind the shack and found the steel drum.

Johnson began handing me sticks of dynamite until they were all in the drum.

I was sweating heavily enough to put a fire out with, but not an oil well fire. Now, the tricky part was at hand. The heavy barrel had to be slid as closely as possible to the fire. I found a long piece of lumber that had been left over from building the shack. It was only about ten feet long, but it would have to do. I also found a piece of steel roofing that I could use as a shield.

I began to move the barrel away from the shack. To what little advantage I had, the ground was downhill and unobstructed toward the well head. I got down on my belly and began pushing the barrel toward the burning oil. I passed insects burned to a crisp and even a roasted rattlesnake as I shoved the barrel before me. Inch by inch, I pushed ever closer to the inferno.

The intensity of the heat was nearly unbearable. The steel roofing strip was like having a hot baking pan on top of me. I'd surely be nursing burns if I survived. Nevertheless, I continued to inch forward, forcing myself to get the barrel close enough so the dynamite could do its job. It occurred to me that I had no idea when the barrel would be close enough.

I was holding that thought and had pushed the dynamite-filled steel barrel to within a couple of feet of the fire, when…

# EPILOGUE

THE NUECES STRIP of 1900 was still mostly a vast prairie of tall grasses and loamy-sands stretching far as the eye could see and beyond. Grasses tended to grow high enough to reach a horse's withers, though stands of live oak, mesquite, and prickly pear cactus brought to the prairie from the south, mostly by seed-carrying birds and by cattle droppings, had already begun to proliferate. Winds blowing through the wiregrass created their own special music. Brush proliferated, often creating nearly impenetrable barriers owing to the density and occasional thorniness.

The Nueces Strip, called "Wild Horse Desert" by some, reached south from the lazily flowing Nueces River all the way to the meandering Rio Grande along Texas' southern border. Its eastern extremity enjoyed the sea breezes wafting in off the Gulf of Mexico from Corpus Christi all the way to Brownsville. Nestled in hills at its northern extreme was the little town of Uvalde, while the semi-arid rolling terrain of Laredo was generally regarded as its far western reach. Rough but serviceable roads were being carved out of the Strip and mostly paralleled the railroads, which continued to proliferate. Texas enjoyed a veritable steel spider web of interconnecting railroads. A form of creative destruction was in full flower.

Despite its mostly uninviting landscape, South Texas drew all sorts of opportunists like moths to a light bulb. Texas still remained a prime destination for second chancers, folks who'd met with rough times and looked to restart their lives. Towns, farms, and ranches sprang up at record pace. They were pressed to conquer a challenging terrain.

Much Texas history centers around the Nueces Strip. No discussion of it can ever be complete without mention that much of the most significant fighting of the Texas War for Independence was fought on and just north of the Nueces Strip back in 1835 and 1836. It was also the scene of the first skirmishes of the Mexican-American War of 1846. The Strip was officially ceded to the United States by the Treaty of Guadalupe Hidalgo in 1848, though Texas had already laid claim.

The plentiful and accessible longhorn were for years the "low-hanging-fruit" of the Nueces Strip economy. They were a hardy breed that could withstand the South Texas heat, fend off disease-carrying pests, and carry just enough meat on their bones to make them reasonably profitable to raise. Originally brought from the Iberian Peninsula by early Spanish priests, the longhorns eventually escaped the mostly failing missionaries, proliferated, and roamed wild and free across the prairies. Millions of the beasts soon covered Texas and especially the excellent grazing lands of the Nueces Strip. They competed with those wild mustangs that had also been introduced by the Spaniards.

Ranchers were increasingly importing and breeding meatier, shorter-horned breeds like Brahmans, Angus,

Herefords, and even Richard King's Santa Gertrudis. Of course, there had been the indigenous buffalo, millions of the beasts. They'd been a staple of the Comanche peoples' way of life until their hides were taken in wholesale slaughters to enrich eastern merchants and scions of fashion. The Texas prairies nevertheless provided plenty of feed for all.

The factor that would ultimately win the west was the family; the larger the better, as children grew up in the face of all manner of lurking dangers. Families established the ranches and farms popping up not only throughout the eastern portions of the Nueces Strip but across Texas as a whole. People sought fresh opportunity. The territory east of the 98th meridian sliced through the very heart of Texas, which was fast becoming an economic juggernaut, and the Strip was no exception. Its economy was based on growing cotton and raising cattle and horses. Cotton was bundled and hauled to port for transport to markets in Louisiana and points east, while cattle were driven mostly to Texas slaughterhouses. And black gold gushing from countless oil wells would soon rise to be a major part of the Texas economy. Indians were pushed ever westward and to reservations, as tribes were overcome by a cocktail of socioeconomic forces, violent conflict, disease, and vast numbers of White settlers.

While the frontier grew ever westward, there remained ongoing worry about the threats posed by rogue off-reservation Comanche, Kiowa, and Lipan Apache, as well as the marauding bandits from south of the Rio Grande and lawbreaking opportunists from the east like the Irish Mob. This all served to keep early Texans on this wild and often lawless frontier ever vigilant. It was easy to make the case for calling up companies of Texas Rangers to patrol the Nueces Strip, as they took it upon themselves to go where the military found it politically undesirable. On the other hand, the legislators in the state capital in Austin often were unable to pull together the financial means to fund the necessary companies of Rangers. They had to rely on the US Army, which could be chancy at best, as it was subject to the politics of whoever was in power and the perceiving of real or imagined threats.

Thus, the setting for the Tumbleweed Sagas: Junior's Story series is hardly any less challenging than mere decades before. Yet civilization marches inexorably onward, taming the remaining frontier.

# A LOOK AT BOOK THIRTEEN

## TEXAS TRUTHS: CRUDE JUSTICE

**Black gold and blood don't mix well on the Nueces.**

Having hung up his badge and kept his promise to Cassie, Texas Ranger Lucas Dunn, Jr. is building something new—a life, a legacy, and a future beneath the South Texas sky. But when oil erupts on the ranch, so does the violence that seems to follow Junior wherever he rides. Apache warrior Tochin strikes the drilling site with savage fury, triggering a blowout that turns fortune into catastrophe.

Junior barely douses the flames before a deeper treachery surfaces. His own oil manager has vanished with the profits—and the trail leads straight into a ruthless crime syndicate bleeding the oil fields dry. No badge. No backup. Just a man who knows what justice looks like.

As crude ambition collides with frontier law, Junior must decide how far he'll ride when everything he's built is at stake. Death doesn't care if you've retired.

***AVAILABLE MAY 2026***

# ACKNOWLEDGMENTS

Authoring books simply doesn't happen in a vacuum. The author provides the creative talent and crafts the stories, but there's so much more that demands acknowledgment. There's lots of folks and places that contribute to my authoring endeavors. So, it is with *Pale Horse of the Apocalypse: Justice Defies Death.* It begins in 1900. The newly wrought exploits of the son of legendary Texas Ranger Captain Luke Dunn were at the core of the Sagas, but the Junior's Story series stands apart.

Lucas Dunn, Junior, symbolizes the lawman image, the pursuer of law and order in the person of a hero, protector, knight-errant sort of character. But there's much more to him. He carries on a family legacy of grit, tenacity, rugged individualism, and bravery, nuanced with a masculine vulnerability and a search for redeeming values. He epitomizes the freedom of America's western frontier and represents a final bastion of honor in America. Hopefully, readers will find *Pale Horse of the Apocalypse: Justice Defies Death* an adventure worthy of their time and emotional involvement. Importantly, Luke is an achiever, a man with purpose.

I've been blessed with many friends and family who have supported my writings. My wife Carolyn's reviews and encouragement were a huge help, along with very important tech support from our sons Mike and Matt. Other supporters have included Cara Miller, Jim May, Ernie Angell, Chris Haug, and my dear cousins Johnny Dunn, Jim

& Cindy Holmgreen, Francette Meaney, and Eddie and Nancy Thornton. Many more friends have contributed support at some level to the creation and publication of my books, including this *Pale Horse of the Apocalypse: Justice Defies Death,* be it encouragement or advice.

Naturally, I am major grateful to the great folks at Wolfpack Publishing. The team they bring to publishing is first rate, from editing to typesetting to cover design and the myriad tasks that lead to successful book sales.

It's only right to acknowledge my ancestors who were actual settlers of the South Texas frontier. In addition to inspiring me, they provided a quite helpful true-to-life framework as to the life and times on the Texas Nueces Strip. It was appropriate to weave them into the tapestry of my western novels. Matthew Dunn (1809-1863) immigrated to Corpus Christi from County Kildare in 1845, established a homestead on Upriver Road in Nuecestown, and served as a sutler to General Zachary Taylor's Army in the Mexican-American War. Peter Dunn (1807-1890) immigrated from Ireland in 1850 and established a blacksmith shop in Corpus Christi.

My great-great-great-grandfather, John Dunn (1803-1889), ranched and grew thousands of acres of cotton; Lawrence Dunn (1837-1864) fought and died with Captain Ware's Confederate cavalry; and my great-great-grandfather Nicholas Dunn (1835-1912) was a rancher, drover, livestock speculator, marksman, and Comanche fighter of some repute. My cousin John Beamond "Red John" Dunn (1851-1940) served as a Texas Ranger in the 1870s under Captain Bland Chamberlain (Company H), subsequently joined a "vigilance committee," became a farmer and merchant, and curated a museum of military weapons displayed to this day in the Corpus Christi Museum of Science & History.

Red John Dunn's brother, Matthew Dunn, also served as

a Texas Ranger, and another cousin, Rut Evans, served as a Texas Ranger in the 1890s (Company E, Frontier Battalion, Alice, TX). My cousin Patrick Dunn was quite successful at raising longhorns on North Padre Island east of Corpus Christi from 1883 to 1937. John Hillard Dunn (1883-1958), whose personal narrative about his family and his own adventures drove my pursuit of my Texas family legacy, inspired my own writings, and led me to write his yet-to-be-published biography, *Tough Hombre: Recollections of a True Texan*. Finally, my grandfather, Horace Charles Greathouse, served as a Texas Ranger in 1920 (Company C, Austin, TX). Such real-life characters, coupled with actual events, have served to reinforce the historical settings for my writings.

Most of my authoring has occurred in my office as decorated to channel my inner Texan, but my creative juices have often been inspired, and my imagination stoked in cafés and coffee houses across America. My favorites were Hester's Café & Coffee Bar in Corpus Christi, TX; Nueces Café in Robstown, TX; Java Ranch Espresso Bar & Café in Fredericksburg, TX; PAX Coffee & Goods in Kerrville, TX; Ragged Edge Coffee House and Bantam Coffee Roasters in Gettysburg, PA; 1889 Coffee House in Helena, MT; Wild Joe's Coffee Shop, Bozeman, MT; Tumbleweed Café, Gardiner, MT; Dunn Brothers Coffee in Rapid City, SD; Postmasters Coffee & Bakery and Brio Coffeehouse in Waynesboro, PA; Birdie's Café and American Ice Co Café in Westminster, MD; Deja Brew Coffee House, New Oxford and Deja Brew at Miney Branch, Carroll Valley, PA; Baltimore Coffee & Tea Co., Frederick Coffee Company & Café, and Dublin Roasters in Frederick, MD; Qualle Café and Grounded Coffee & Bakery, Cherokee, NC; Palace Café, Amarillo, TX; and Unto Others Café, Lamar, CO. I must admit to also frequenting a few Dunkin Donuts and Starbucks around our fine nation. The décors and easy listening music in these fine establishments, combined with savory cups of coffee, tended to set me in the right creative frame of mind. They also afforded engagement with many fine citizens of our nation.

Last but not least, I'm especially thankful for the many folks who have read and enjoyed my books, be it print, digital, or audio.

I do believe it is important to acknowledge how the old west represents the brave pioneering spirit of settlers who met the challenges and transcended mere survival to enable America to achieve exceptional growth. The settling of the American west is replete with tales of leveraging freedom for individual achievement. I hope you will agree that reliving our past—even through history-based fiction—often has the effect of pointing the way to an ever-brighter future. Might we be up to it? I hope that the inspiration I have drawn from my having walked the very earth my characters have trodden, coupled with my extensive historical research, will enable readers to fully experience the grit, adventure, and passion of my characters while sensing aromas of gunsmoke, trail dust, leather, sweat, and bluebonnets.

Thanks kindly to all of you, and do enjoy *Pale Horse of the Apocalypse: Justice Defies Death.*

# ABOUT THE AUTHOR

Multiple-award-winning author Mark Greathouse is a fifth-generation Texan devoted to history and writing western genre fiction. He has published fourteen western novels, an anthology, and a biography, as well as published western history articles in various magazines and newspapers. He received a 2025 Western Writers of America Spur Finalist Award for Short Fiction with "Prairie Dog" published in a local anthology. *Guns on the Guadalupe: Justice on the River,* published by Wolfpack Publishing, continues Greathouse's passion for weaving fiction in a historical setting. He crafts an engaging adventure, featuring an ensemble of captivating characters woven into compellingly complex subplots. Importantly, he has stayed true to the western story being America's morality story, as good triumphs over evil. Whether expressed in his epic western genre novels or adventure-laced biographies, he couples a soul-penetrating creative spirit with extensive historical research that attracts a broad spectrum of readers. Greathouse is a member of Western Writers of America and several poetry societies. He holds BA and MBA degrees. Greathouse lives in Southern Pennsylvania but travels west regularly to walk in the footsteps of his characters.

www.ingramcontent.com/pod-product-compliance
Lightning Source LLC
LaVergne TN
LVHW040218110826
845146LV00005B/1339
* 9 7 9 8 8 9 5 6 7 3 2 1 8 *